The Hollywood Hills Clinic

Where doctors to the stars work miracles by day—
and explore their hearts' desires by night...

When hotshot doc James Rothsberg started the clinic
six years ago he dreamed of a world-class facility, catering
to Hollywood's biggest celebrities, and his team are
unrivalled in their fields. Now, as the glare of the media
spotlight grows, the Hollywood Hills Clinic is teaming up
with the pro-bono Bright Hope Clinic, and James is reunited
with Dr Mila Brightman...the woman he jilted at the altar!

When it comes to juggling the care of Hollywood A-listers
with care for the underprivileged kids of LA *anything* can
happen...and sizzling passions run high in the shadow of
the red carpet. With everything at stake for James, Mila
and the Hollywood Hills Clinic medical team,
their biggest challenges have only just begun!

Find out what happens in the dazzling
The Hollywood Hills Clinic miniseries:

Seduced by the Heart Surgeon
by Carol Marinelli

Falling for the Single Dad
by Emily Forbes

Tempted by Hollywood's Top Doc
by Louisa George

Perfect Rivals...
by Amy Ruttan

The Prince and the Midwife
by Robin Gianna

His Pregnant Sleeping Beauty
by Lynne Marshall

And look out for another two titles from
The Hollywood Hills Clinic next month!

Dear Reader,

It's always fun to be part of a continuity with seven other authors—especially such a talented group! When I met my characters Joseph and Carey I immediately fell in love. Joe is the kind of hero you want to throw your arms around and never let go. The problem is he doesn't want to let anyone close enough to do that. He has his reasons, believe me, and they're doozies. Carey is a glass-half-full kind of girl, even though life has thrown her some tough issues with which to deal. From the moment Joe sees Carey he assigns himself as her guardian—and what a lucky girl she becomes! I rooted for their happily-ever-after right from the start!

His Pregnant Sleeping Beauty is the first time I've ever written about a paramedic hero. Fortunately I had some wonderful personal resources, and therefore I feel my scenes are authentic. In fact you could say I'm proud of them. What a tough job first responders have! And writing about Carey took me back to my RN roots. I just love nurse heroines! So I guess you could call me a happy camper all round, being the lucky lady to write their story in Book 6 of The Hollywood Hills Clinic series. Why not check them all out?

Dear readers, if you read a book and enjoy it please consider writing a short review to help spread the word. Or give a shout-out about it on social media. We authors really appreciate that. Oh, and if you're on Facebook 'friend' me, I'd love to keep in touch.

Until next time,

Lynne

PS Visit my website to keep up with all the news: lynnemarshall.com. You can also sign up for my author newsletter there.

HIS PREGNANT
SLEEPING
BEAUTY

BY
LYNNE MARSHALL

Published in Great Britain 2016
By Mills & Boon, an imprint of HarperCollins*Publishers*
1 London Bridge Street, London, SE1 9GF

© 2016 Harlequin Books S.A.

*Special thanks and acknowledgement are given to Lynne Marshall
for her contribution to* The Hollywood Hills Clinic *series*

ISBN: 978-0-263-06472-8

Lynne Marshall used to worry that she had a serious problem with daydreaming—then she discovered she was supposed to *write* those stories! A Registered Nurse for twenty-six years, she came to fiction-writing later than most. Now she writes romance which usually includes medicine, but always comes straight from her heart. She is happily married, a Southern California native, a woman of faith, a dog-lover, an avid reader, a curious traveller and a proud grandma.

Books by Lynne Marshall

Mills & Boon Medical Romance

Cowboys, Doctors…Daddies!

Hot-Shot Doc, Secret Dad
Father For Her Newborn Baby

Temporary Doctor, Surprise Father
The Boss and Nurse Albright
The Heart Doctor and the Baby
The Christmas Baby Bump
Dr Tall, Dark…and Dangerous?
NYC Angels: Making the Surgeon Smile
200 Harley Street: American Surgeon in London
A Mother for His Adopted Son

Visit the Author Profile page
at millsandboon.co.uk for more titles.

This book is dedicated to the two paramedics
who helped me make my character, Joe, a true hero.
Thank you, John-Philip Maarschalk
and Rick Ochocki, for your expert input and help.
What would the world be without our first responders?

CHAPTER ONE

CAREY SPENCER HAD never felt more alone in her life than when she got off the bus in Hollywood.

Joseph Matthews, on that night's shift for the prestigious Hollywood Hills Clinic, had just delivered one of the industry's favorite character actresses to the exclusive twenty-bed extended recovery hotel. It was tucked between Children's Hospital and a smaller private hospital on Sunset Boulevard, and the common eye would never guess its function. Joe had agreed to make the Wednesday night run because James Rothsberg himself had asked. After all, the lady *had* won an award for Best Supporting Actress the year before last.

As the lead paramedic for the ambulance line he owned, Joe had attended the not-to-be-named-aloud patient during the uneventful ride to the recovery hotel. She'd been heavily sedated, her IV was in place, her vitals, including oxygen saturation, were fine, but she'd had so much work done on her face, breasts and hands she looked like a mummy. When they'd arrived, you'd have thought he'd delivered the President to Walter Reed National Military Medical Center the way the abundant staff rushed to the ambulance and took over the transfer.

Now, at nine p.m., back sitting in the front of the private ambulance, Joe switched on some music. Jazz, his favorite station. Yeah, he owned this bus—hell, he owned all six of them—so he could play whatever music he wanted. But that also kept him thinking about work a lot. It was the first of the month and he'd have to make copies of the June shift schedule for the EMTs and paramedics on his team before they showed up for work tomorrow morning.

"I'm hungry," Benny, his EMT, said from behind the wheel.

Why was Joe not surprised? The kid had barely turned twenty and seemed to have hollow legs.

Restless and out of sorts, a state that was nothing new these days, Joe nodded. "How about that Mexican grill?" They'd just made their last run on Friday night, without plans for later, so why not?

"You read my mind." Benny tossed him a cockeyed grin, his oversized Afro flopping with the quick movement.

He turned off Hollywood Boulevard and up N. Cahuenga to the fast-food place by the cross-country bus depot, where a bus had just arrived from Who Knew Where, USA. Benny had to wait to pull into a larger-than-average parking space. Joe mindlessly watched a handful of people trickle off the bus.

A damn fine-looking young woman wearing oversized sunglasses got off. Sunglasses at night. What was up with that? She was slender and her high-heeled boots made her look on the tall side. She wore jeans and a dark blue top, or was it a sweater? Her thick hair was layered and long with waves and under the bus depot lights looked brown. Reddish? He wondered what her story was. Probably because of the shades at night. But he didn't bother to think about ladies these days. Yet, still, dang, she was hot. And stood out like a rose in a thorn patch.

Benny backed the private ambulance into the space at the farthest end of the restaurant lot, and Joe got out the passenger side, immediately getting hit by the mouthwatering aroma of spicy beans and chipotle chicken. He stretched, eager to chow down. A sudden movement in his peripheral vision drew his attention. Someone sprang from behind a pillar and snagged a lady's purse strap and wrist, pulling her out of the crowd and toward the nearby alley. It was the woman he'd just been gawking at! The other travelers had mostly dispersed. She put up a fight, too, and squealed, yet the few people left lingering didn't seem to notice…but he did.

Joe ran to the mouth of the alley. "Hey!" Then sprinted toward the young woman, who was still fighting to hold on to her purse.

The tall but skinny, straggly-haired dude dragged her by the shoulder strap and wrist deeper down the alley. *Why doesn't she just let go? Ah, wait, it's one of those over-the-torso jobs.*

"Hey!"

This time the guy turned and whacked her with his fist, knocking the young woman to the ground. Her head hit with a thud. He ripped off the purse, hitting her head on the pavement again, then stepped over her to get to Joe with a wild swing.

Joe blocked the first punch with little effort—the dumb punk didn't know what he was dealing with as he boxed for his workouts—but the guy pulled a knife and lashed out. Joe threw another punch and landed it, even while feeling a hot lightning-quick slice across his ribs. Now he was really ticked. The guy ran deeper into the alley with Joe in pursuit, soon disappearing over a large trash bin and tall crumbling brick wall. Joe skidded to a brief stop and watched in disbelief. For a scumbag the man was agile. Probably from a lot of practice in assaulting innocent people.

The girl! Holding his side, he sprinted back to where she lay. Out cold.

Benny met up with him. "I called the police. You okay?"

"Just a superficial wound." Still, he checked it briefly since an adrenaline rush could mask pain. The last thing he wanted to find out was that the cut was deep enough to cause evisceration and he hadn't noticed. Fortunately the only thing he saw was oozing blood, nothing gushing. He'd throw a thick absorbent pad over his middle as soon as Benny got back with the trauma kit, oxygen bag and backboard. He didn't want to bleed all over the poor lady. "Bring our equipment, okay?" He grabbed a pair of gloves from Benny's belt, and knelt in front of the young woman as Benny took off for the ambulance. "I'm a paramedic, miss. Are you okay?" he said loudly and clearly. She didn't respond.

She'd hit her head hard when she'd fallen—correct that, had been punched to the ground. He tried to rouse her with a firm hand on her shoulder. "Hello? You okay, you awake, miss?"

He watched the rise and fall of her chest. At least she was breathing normally. He felt her neck for the carotid pulse and found it. Rate and strength normal. Good. He scanned her body for bleeding or other signs of obvious injury. Maybe the scumbag had stabbed her too. Then he used the palms of his gloved hands to sweep the underside of her arms and legs to check for bleeding, and did the same beneath both sides of her back. So far so good.

There was a fifty-cent-sized pool of blood behind her head, but he didn't move her neck, not before he and Benny had placed a cervical collar on her. Her assailant had run off with her purse and she didn't appear to have any other form of ID. He checked her wrist and then her neck to see if she wore any emergency alert jewelry. No such luck. They'd have to wait until she regained consciousness to find out who she was.

Even under the dim lights in the alley she had an obvious black eye, and because the dirtbag had yanked off her torso-anchored purse strap the sweater she'd been wearing had been pulled halfway down her left arm... which was covered in bruises. She'd just been mugged, but these marks weren't fresh. Anger surged through him. She'd been beaten up long before today.

What kind of guy treated a woman like that?

He shook his head. Of all the lousy luck. She hadn't stepped off the bus five minutes ago and had already gotten mugged and knocked unconscious. The only thing she had going for her on this nightmare of a Friday night was him. He shuddered for the young stranger over what might have played out if he hadn't been here.

Maybe it was those thick eyelashes that seemed to glue her eyes shut, or her complete vulnerability, being unconscious in an alley, or maybe it was the obvious signs of abuse, but for whatever reason Joe was suddenly struck with an uncompromising need to protect her.

From this moment on tonight he vowed to take responsibility for the out-of-luck Jane Doe. Hell, if anyone had ever needed a guardian angel, she did.

Benny had moved the ambulance closer, and brought the backboard and equipment. Joe let Benny apply a large sloppy dressing around his middle as he checked her airway again, noting she had good air exchange. He worried, with the head injury, that she might vomit and wanted to be near if she did to prevent aspiration.

"We're going to give you some oxygen and put a collar round your neck," Joe said calmly, hoping she might already be regaining consciousness and hear him explain everything they did to her. They worked together and soon had Jane on the backboard for stability. Joe secured her with the straps, never taking his eyes off her. She had definitely been knocked out cold, yet still breathed evenly. A good thing. But he knew when unconscious people woke up they could often be combative and try to take off the oxygen and cervical collar. Hell, after what she'd just been through, could he blame her if she woke up fighting?

With her long dark auburn hair spread over her shoulders and her hands strapped to the transport board, she made the strangest image.

An urban Sleeping Beauty.

"Ready for transfer?" Joe said, breaking his own thoughts.

"Don't you want to wait for the police?"

"If they're not here by the time we get her in the back of the van, you call them again and tell them to meet us at the clinic. She might have a skull fracture or subdural bleed for all we know, and needs medical attention ASAP." He knew the next forty-five minutes were all she had remaining in the golden hour for traumatic head injury. "I'm going to call Dr. Rothsberg and let him know what we've got."

He jumped into the back of the van first to guide the head of the gurney on which they'd placed the long spine board and patient as Benny pushed from the back, then he rolled the gurney forward and locked it in place with sprung locks on the ambulance floor.

He'd ride in the back with her. If she woke up, confused and possibly combative, he wanted to be there. Plus it would be his chance to do a more thorough examination.

Joe did another assessment of Sleeping Beauty's condition. Unchanged. Then he made the call. Unexpectedly, Dr. Rothsberg said to bring her to the clinic instead of county. Which was a good thing, because Joe would have taken her home before he'd consider delivering a Jane Doe to county hospital to potentially slip through every conceivable crack due to their overstretched system.

He stripped off the makeshift dressing and his shirt to assess his own wound, which was long and jagged, still wept blood and would definitely need stitches. Now that he was looking at it, it burned like hell. Benny had a short conversation with the police, who'd just arrived. Great timing! He showed them where they'd found her and where the attacker had fled over the wall then left them to look for witnesses as Joe cleaned and dressed his own wound. Damn, the disinfectant smarted! One of the policemen took a quick look inside the ambulance, saw the victim and Joe with his injury, nodded and took off toward the alley.

Benny closed the back doors of the van, got into the driver's seat then started the ambulance. "They'll take our statements at the clinic later."

"Good," Joe said, taping his dressing, constantly checking his patient as he did so.

As Benny drove, with their lights flashing, Joe checked her vital signs again, this time using a blood-pressure cuff then a stethoscope to listen to her lungs.

He opened her eyes, opening the blackened eye more gingerly, and used his penlight to make sure she hadn't blown a pupil. Fortunately she hadn't, but unfortunately he'd had to move a clump of her hair away from her face in order to do so. It was thick and wavy, and, well, somehow it felt too intimate, touching it. It'd been a while since he'd run his fingers through a woman's hair, which he definitely wasn't doing right now, but the thought of wanting to bothered him.

By the status of her black eye, it'd been there a few days and definitely looked ugly and intentional. Someone had punched her. That was a fact. There was that anger again, flaming out of nowhere for a woman he knew zero about.

He decided to insert a hep-lock into her antecubital fossa so the clinic would have a line ready to go on arrival. A head injury could increase cranial pressure and so could IV fluid. He didn't want to add to that, and so far her blood pressure was within normal limits. While he performed the tasks he thought about everything that had happened to his patient prior to winding up in that alley.

She'd gotten off the bus and hadn't waited to collect a suitcase, which meant all she'd carried with her was in that large shoulder bag. And that was long gone with the punk who'd knocked her cold and jumped the wall. He tightened his fists. What he'd give to deck that guy and leave him in some alley.

If Joe added up the clues he'd guess that the lovely Sleeping Jane was running from whoever had bruised her arms and blackened her eye. She'd probably grabbed whatever she could and snuck away from…

"Who are you?" Joe asked quietly, wondering if she could hear him, knowing that unconscious people sometimes still heard what went on around them. "Where did you come from?"

He lifted one of her hands, that fierce sense of protectiveness returning, and held it in his, noticing the long thin fingers with carefully manicured but unpainted nails, and made another silent vow. *Don't worry, I'll look out for you. You don't have to be afraid where I'm taking you.*

They arrived at The Hollywood Hills Clinic, nestled far beneath the Hollywood sign at the end of narrow winding roads with occasional hairpin turns. The swanky private clinic that hugged the hillside always reminded him of something Frank Lloyd Wright might have designed for the twenty-first century, if he were still alive. The stacked boxy levels of the modern stone architecture, nearly half of it made of special earthquake-resistant glass, looked like a diamond in the night on the hillside. Warm golden light glowed from every oversized window, assuring the private clinic was open twenty-four hours. For security and privacy purposes, there were tall fences out front, and a gate every vehicle had to clear, except for ambulances. They breezed through as soon as the gate opened completely.

Benny headed toward the private patient loading area at the back of the building. Joe put his shirt back on and gingerly buttoned it over his bandaged and stinging rib cage.

He still couldn't believe his good fortune over landing the bid as the private ambulance company for James Rothsberg's clinic only two short years after starting his own business. He'd been an enterprising twenty-three-year-old paramedic with a plan back then, thanks to a good mind for business instilled in him by his hard-working father. James must have seen something about him he liked when he'd interviewed him and Joe had tendered his bid. Or maybe it had had more to do with the nasty info leak the previous ambulance company had been responsible for, exposing several of the A-list actors in the biz on a TV gossip show, making Joe's timing impeccable. He used to think of it as fate.

James's parents—Michael Rothsberg and Aubrey St. Claire—had had enough info leaks in their lives to fill volumes. Everyone, even Joe, remembered the scandal, and he'd only been in his early teens at the time. Their stories had made headlines on every supermarket rag and cable TV talk show. Everyone knew about their private affairs. After all, James's parents had been Hollywood royalty, and had been two of the highest-paid actors in the business. Watching them fall from grace had become a national pastime after a nasty kiss-and-tell book by an ex-lover had outed them as phonies. Their marriage had been a sham, and their teenage children, James and Freya, had suffered most.

James had told Joe on the day he'd hired him that loyalty to the clinic and the patients was the number-one rule, he wouldn't tolerate anything less, and Joe had lived up to that pledge every single day he'd shown up to work. He'd walked out of James's office that day thinking fate was on his side and he was the luckiest man on earth, but he too would soon experience his own fall. Like James, it hadn't been of his own making but that didn't mean it had hurt any less.

These days Joe didn't believe in fate or luck. No, he'd changed his thinking on that and now, for him, everything happened for a reason. Even his damned infertility, which he was still trying to figure out. He glanced at the hand where his wedding ring had once been but didn't let himself go there, instead focusing on the positive. The here and now. The new contract. His job security.

The clinic had opened its doors six years ago, and two years later, right around the time James's sister Freya had joined the endeavor, Joe's private ambulance service had been the Rothsbergs' choice for replacement. Having just signed a new five-year contract with the clinic, Joe almost thought of himself as another Hollywood success story. Hell, he was only twenty-eight, owned his own business, and worked for the most revered clinic in town.

But how could he call it true success when the rest of his life was such a mess?

James Rothsberg himself met the ambulance, along with another doctor and a couple of nurses, and Joe prepared to transfer his sleeping beauty.

A little bit taller than Joe, James's strong and well-built frame matched Joe's on the fitness scale. Where they parted ways was in the looks department. The son of A-list actors, James was what the gossip magazines called "an Adonis in scrubs". Yeah, he was classy, smooth and slick. He was the man every woman dreamed of and every man wanted to be, and Joe wasn't afraid to admit he had a man crush on the guy. Strictly platonic, of course, based on pure admiration. The doctor ran the lavish clinic for the mind-numbingly affluent, who flocked to him, eager to pay the price for his plastic surgery services. Well, someone had to support the outrageously luxurious clinic and the well-paid staff. In fact, someone on staff had recently commented after a big awards ceremony that half of the stars in attendance had been through the clinic's doors. A statement that wasn't far from the truth.

"James, what are you still doing here?"

"You piqued my interest," James said. "I had to see Jane Doe for myself."

Joe pushed the gurney out of the back of the ambulance, and Rick, one of the evening nurses, pulled from the other end.

James studied Jane Doe as she rolled by. "She didn't get that shiner tonight."

"Nope," Joe said. "There's a whole other story that went down before she got mugged."

James nodded agreement. "That reminds me, I got a call from the police department. They'll be here shortly to take your statement." He tugged Joe by the arm. "Let's take a look at your injury before they get here, okay?"

Joe was torn between looking after Sleeping Beauty or himself, but knew the clinic staff would give her the utmost medical attention. Besides, it wasn't every day the head of the clinic offered to give one-to-one patient care to an employee.

"Thanks, Doc. I really appreciate it."

"It's totally selfish. I've got to look out for my lead paramedic, right?" James said in a typically self-deprecating manner. That was another thing he liked so much about the guy. He never flaunted his wealth or his status.

Joe glanced across the room at the star patient of the night, Ms. Jane Doe, still unconscious but breathing steadily, and felt a little tug in his chest, then followed James into an examination room.

After the nursing assistant removed Joe's dressing, James studied it. "So what happened here?"

Joe explained what had transpired in the alley as the doctor applied pressure to one area that continued to bleed.

"Oh, you're definitely getting a tetanus shot. Who knows what was on that guy's blade."

"Well, he *was* a scumbag."

"Good thing you've got a trained plastic surgeon to stitch you up. I'd hate to ruin those perfect washboard abs."

Joe laughed, knowing his rigorous workout sessions plus boxing kept him fit. Boxing had been the one thing he could do to keep sane and not beat the hell out of his best friend during his divorce. "Ouch," he said, surprised by how sensitive his wound was as the nursing assistant cleaned the skin.

"Ouch!" he repeated, when the first topical anesthetic was injected by James.

The doctor chuckled. "Man up, dude. I'm just getting started."

That got an ironic laugh out of Joe. *Yeah, sterile dude, man up!*

"You won't be feeling much in a couple of minutes."

Joe knew the drill, he'd sutured his share of patients in his field training days, but this was the first time in his entire life he'd been the patient in need of stitches. Hell, he'd never even needed a butterfly bandage before.

"So, about the girl with the black eye," James said, donning sterile gloves while preparing the small sterile minor operations tray. "I wonder if she may have had any prior intracranial injuries that might have contributed to her immediately falling unconscious."

"I was wondering the same thing, but she hit that pavement really hard. I hope she doesn't have a subdural hematoma."

"We're doing a complete head trauma workup on her."

"Thanks. I know this probably sounds weird, but

I feel personally responsible for her, having seen the whole thing go down, not getting there fast enough, and being the first to treat her and all. Especially since she doesn't have any ID."

"You broke a rule, right? Got involved with your patient?"

"Didn't mean to, but I guess you could say that. I know it's foolish—"

James turned back toward him. "And this might be foolish too, but when the police come we'll tell them we'll be treating *and* letting our Jane Doe recover right here."

Touched beyond words, as the cost for staying at this exclusive clinic would be astronomical, Joe wanted to shake the good doctor's hand but he wore sterile gloves. "Thank you. I really—" He was about to say "appreciate that" but quickly went quiet, not used to being the patient as the first stitch was placed, using a nasty-looking hooked needle, and though he didn't feel anything, he still didn't want to move.

"If I stitch this up just so, there'll hardly be a scar. On the other hand, I could make you look like you've got a seven pack."

As the saying went, it only hurt when he laughed.

A couple of hours later, the police had taken a thorough report, and also told Joe they hadn't found anyone matching the description a couple of witnesses had given for the suspect, they also said they hadn't recovered Jane Doe's purse.

Joe sighed and shook his head. She'd continue to be Madam X until she came to. Which hopefully would be soon.

"We do have one lead, though."

He glanced up, hopeful whatever that lead was it might point to Jane's identity.

"The clinic staff found a bus-ticket stub in her sweater pocket. If she used a credit card to purchase the ticket, we might be able to trace it back and identify her."

"That's great. But what if she paid cash?"

"That might imply she didn't want to be traced."

"Probably explain those bruises, too."

The cop nodded. "The most we could possibly find out is the origin of the ticket. Which city she boarded in, but she's bound to wake up soon, right?"

Joe glanced across the room. Jane was now in one of the clinic's fancy hospital gowns and hooked up to an IV, still looking as peaceful as a sleeping child. "It's hard to say with concussion and potential brain swelling. The doctors may determine she needs surgery for a subdural hematoma or something, for all I know."

The young cop looked grim as he considered that possibility, and Joe was grateful for his concern. "Well, we'll be in touch." He gave Joe his card. "If she wakes up, or if there's anything you remember or want to talk about, give me a call. Likewise, I'll let you know if we find anything out."

"Thanks."

An orderly and RN rolled Jane by Joe. "Where's she going?"

"To her room in the DOU. She's in Seventeen A."

The definitive observation unit was for the patients who needed extra care. Dr. Di Williams ran the unit like a well-oiled machine. Jane would be well looked after, but... He made a snap decision—he wasn't going home tonight. If James and Di would let him, he'd wait things out right here.

Fifteen minutes later, Sleeping Beauty was tucked into a high-end single bed in a room that looked more like one in a luxury spa hotel than a hospital. The only thing giving it away were the bedside handrails and the stack of monitors camouflaged in the corner with huge vases and flower arrangements. The tasteful beige, white and cream decor was relaxing, but Joe couldn't sleep. Instead, he sat in the super-comfy bedside chair resting his head in the palm of his right hand, watching *her* sleep. Wondering what her story was, and pondering why he felt so responsible for her. He decided it was because she was completely vulnerable. He knew the feeling. Someone besides a staff nurse had to look out for her until they found out who she was and could locate her family.

Sporting that black eye and those healing bruises on her arms, it was likely she had been in an abusive relationship. Most likely she'd been beaten up by the man she'd thought she loved.

His left thumb flicked the inside of his vacant ring finger, reminding him, on a much more personal level, how deeply love could hurt.

CHAPTER TWO

A FIRM HAND sent Joe out of a half dreaming, half awake state. He'd been smiling, floating around somewhere, smiling. The grip on his shoulder made a burst of adrenaline mainline straight to his heart, making his pulse ragged and shaky. He sat bolt upright, his eyes popping open. In less than a second he remembered where he was, turned his head toward the claw still grabbing him, and stared up at the elderly night nurse.

Cecelia, was it?

"What's up?" he said, trying to sound awake, then glancing toward the hospital bed and the patient he'd let down by falling asleep. Some guardian he'd turned out to be. She'd been placed on her side, either sound asleep or still unconscious, with pillows behind her back and between her knees, and he hadn't even woken up.

"Your services are needed," Cecelia said with a grainy voice. "We have a helicopter transfer to Santa Barbara."

"Got it. Take care of her."

"What I'm paid for," Cecelia mumbled, fiddling with the blanket covering her patient.

Joe stood, took one last look at Jane, who still looked peaceful, and walked to the nearest men's room to freshen up, then reported for duty in the patient transitioning room.

Rick, the RN from last night, was at the end of his shift and gave Joe his report. "The fifty-four-year-old patient is status post breast reduction, liposuction and lower face lift. Surgery and overnight recovery were uneventful. She's being transferred to Santa Barbara Cottage Hotel for the remainder of her recovery. IV in right forearm. Last medicated for pain an hour ago with seventy-five milligrams of Demerol. Dressings and drainage tubes in place, no excess bleeding noted. She's been released by Dr. R. for transfer." The male RN, fit and overly tanned, making his blue eyes blaze, gave Joe a deadpan stare. "All systems go. She's all yours." Then, when out of earshot of the patient, Rick whispered, "I didn't vote for her husband."

Joe accompanied the patient and gurney to the waiting helicopter on the roof and loaded the sleeping patient onto the air ambulance. He did a quick head-to-toe assessment before strapping her down and locking the special hydraulic gurney into place. He then made sure any and all emergency equipment was stocked and ready for use. After he hooked up the patient to the heart and BP monitor, he put headphones on his patient first and then himself and took his seat, buckling in, preparing for the noisy helicopter blades to whir to life then takeoff.

After delivering the patient to the Santa Barbara airport and transferring the politician's wife, who would not be named, to the awaiting recovery hotel team, he hoped to grab some coffee and maybe a quick breakfast while they waited for the okay to take off for the return trip.

Two hours later, back at the clinic, Joe's only goal

was to check in on Jane Doe. He hoped she'd come to
and by now maybe everyone knew her name, and he
wondered what it might be. Alexis? Belle? Collette?
Excitedly he dashed into her room and found her as
he'd left her...unconscious. Disappointment buttoned
around him like a too-tight jacket.

The day shift nurse was at her side, preparing to
give her a bed bath. A basin of water sat on the bedside table with steam rising from the surface. Several
towels and cloths and a new patient gown were neatly
stacked beside it. A thick, luxurious patient bath blanket
was draped across her chest, Sleeping Beauty obviously
naked underneath it. He felt the need to look away until
the nurse pulled the privacy curtain around the bed.

"No change?" he asked, already knowing and hating the answer.

"No. But her lab results were a bit of a surprise."

"Everything okay with her skull?"

"Oh, yeah, the CT cranial scan and MRI were both
normal except for the fact she's got one hell of a concussion with brain swelling. Well, along with still being
unconscious and a slow-wave EEG to prove it."

Joe knew the hospital privacy policy, and this nurse
wasn't about to tell him Jane Doe's lab results. Theo-
retically it wasn't any of his business. Except he'd made
a vow last night, and had made it his business to look
after her. As he hadn't signed off on his paramedic admission notes for Jane last night, he suddenly needed
to access her computer chart to do so.

He headed to the intake department to find a vacant computer, but not before running into James, who
looked rested and ready to take on the day. Joe, on the
other hand, had gotten a glimpse of himself in the mirror when he'd made a quick pit stop on arriving back at

the clinic a few minutes earlier. Dark circles beneath his eyes, a day's growth of beard... Yeah, he was a mess.

"What are you still doing here?" James asked.

"Just got back from a helicopter run to Santa Barbara for one of your patients."

"Cecelia told me you stayed here last night."

Damn that night nurse. "Yeah, well, I wanted to be around if Jane Doe woke up."

He didn't look amused. "This is an order, Joe. Go home and get some sleep. Don't come back until your usual evening shift. Got it?"

"Got it. Just have to sign off my charting first."

Several staff members approached James with questions, giving Joe the chance to sneak off to the computer. He logged on and quickly accessed Jane Doe's folder. First he read her CT scan results and the MRI, which were positive for concussion and brain swelling, but without fractures or bleeding, then he took a look at her labs. So far so good. Her drug panel was negative. Good. Her electrolytes, blood glucose, liver and kidney function tests were all within normal limits. Good. Then his gaze settled on a crazy little test result that nearly knocked him out of the chair.

A positive *pregnancy* test.

His suddenly dry-as-paper tongue made it difficult to swallow. His pulse thumped harder and his mind took a quick spin, gathering questions as it did. Did the mystery lady know she was pregnant? He wondered if the father had been worried out of his mind about her since she'd gone missing. Or was the guy who beat her up the father...because she was pregnant?

Had she been running away? Most likely.

Shifting thoughts made bittersweet memories roll through his mind over another most important pregnancy test. One that had changed his life. He wanted more than anything to make those thoughts stop, knowing they never led to a good place, but right now he was too tired to fight them off.

He'd once been on that pregnancy roller-coaster ride, one day ecstatic about the prospect of becoming a father. Another day further down the line getting a different lab test irrefutably stating there was no way in hell he could have gotten his wife pregnant. Any hope of becoming a father had been ripped away. The questions. The confrontations. The ugly answers that had finally torn his marriage apart.

Hell.

He needed to leave the clinic. James had been right. He should go home and get some sleep because if he didn't he might do something he still wanted to do desperately. Give his best—strike that—*ex*-best friend the beating he deserved.

On the third day Joe sat in his now favorite chair at the mystery lady's bedside, thumbing through a fitness magazine. Di Williams, the middle-aged, hardworking head of DOU, had shaken him up earlier when she'd explained Sleeping Beauty's condition as brain trauma—or, in her case, swelling of the brain—that had disconnected the cerebral cortex circuits, kind of like a car idling but not firing up the engine. She'd also said that if she didn't come around soon, they'd have to consider her in a coma and would need to move her to a hospital that could best meet her longer-term needs.

The thought of losing track of the woman he'd vowed to look after made his stomach knot. The doctor had also said she'd be getting transferred to a specialist coma unit later that afternoon for an enhanced CT scan that would test for blood flow and metabolic activity and they'd have to go from there, which kept Joe's stomach feeling tangled and queasy.

Time was running out, and it seemed so unfair for the girl from the bus. What about her baby?

Jane moved and Joe went on alert. It was the first time he'd witnessed what the nurses had said she often did. He'd admitted, when no one had been around, to flicking her cheek with his finger from time to time to get some kind of reaction out of her, but nothing had ever happened. The lady definitely wasn't faking it. She moved again, this time quicker, as though restless. A dry sound emitted from her throat. He held his breath and felt his heart pump faster as he pushed the call light for the attending nurse.

Jane Doe was waking up.

Tiny sputtering electrical fuses seemed to turn on and off inside him as his anticipation grew. He stood, leaned over the hospital bed and watched the sleeping beauty's lids flutter. Instinctively, he turned off the overhead lamp to help decrease the shock of harsh light to her vision as her eyes slowly opened.

They were dark green. And beautiful, like her.

But they'd barely opened before they snapped shut again as her features contorted with fear.

Carey fought for her life, flailing her arms, kicking her feet. Someone wanted to hurt her. It wasn't Ross. Not this time. She ran, but her feet wouldn't move. She tried to scream, but the sound didn't leave her throat. Fear like she'd never felt before consumed her, but she couldn't give up, she had to protect herself in order to protect her baby.

Someone shouted and ran toward her. She knew he

wanted to help. Broad shoulders, and legs moving in a powerful sprint. "Hey!" His voice cut through the night. That face. Strong. Determined. Filled with anger over the man trying to take her purse. She fought more. She had to break away from the smelly man's grip.

"Hey!"

Fight. Fight. Get away.

"Hold on, everything's okay. You're safe." Did she recognize the man's voice? "I've got you." Hands gripped her shoulders, kept her still. She held her breath.

More hands smoothed back her hair. "It's okay, hon." A woman's voice. "Calm down. You're in the hospital."

Hospital? Had she heard right?

Carey shook her head. It hurt. She was hit by a wave of vertigo that made her quit squirming. She lay still, waiting for the hands to release her. It felt like she was in an extremely comfortable bed. She relaxed her tight, squinting eyes and slowly opened first one then the other. She turned her head to a shadow looming above her. It had features. The face she remembered from her dreams. Strong. Brave. Was this *still* a dream?

She stared at him, her breathing rapid, waiting for her eyes to adjust to the light. He was the man who'd taken on her attacker. She scanned his face. Kind brown eyes. Short dark hair. A square jaw. Good looking.

"You're in the hospital and you're safe," he said in a low, comforting voice.

She looked beyond him to a gorgeous room. A hospital? It looked more like an expensive hotel with muted colors and modern furniture, chic, classy, a room she'd never been able to afford in her life. Was she still dreaming? Since she'd stopped protesting, it was quiet. Oh, and there was an IV in her arm. Being an RN herself, she recognized that right off. A catheter between her legs? And she wore a hospital gown. But this one was silky and smooth, not one of those worn-out over-starched jobs at the hospital where she worked.

Everything was so strange. Surreal. As she gathered her senses she couldn't remember where she was other than being in a hospital. She couldn't figure out why she'd be here. Wait. Someone had attacked her. She'd been pushed down. *Oh, no!* Her hand flew to her stomach, and she gasped.

"My baby!" Her voice sounded muffled and strange, as if her ears were plugged.

"Your baby's fine," the woman said. "So you remember you're pregnant."

Her hearing improved. She nodded, and it hurt, but she smiled anyway because her baby was fine.

The attractive young man smiled back at her, and the concern in his eyes was surprising. Did she know him?

"My baby's fine," she whispered to him, and a rush of feelings overcame her until she cried.

Then the strangest thing happened. The man that she wasn't sure if she knew or not, the man with the kind brown eyes…his welled up, too. "Your baby's fine." His voice sounded raspy.

She cried softly for a few moments, his eyes misty and glistening as he gave a caring smile, and it felt so good.

"Where am I?"

"You're in the hospital, hon," the nearby nurse said.

"But *where* am I?"

"Hollywood," he said. "You're in California."

She thought hard, vaguely remembering getting on a bus. Getting off a bus. It was all too much to straighten out right now. She was exhausted.

"What's your name, honey?" The nurse continued.

"Carey Spencer." At least she remembered her name. But she needed to rest. To close her eyes and…

"She's out again." The kind man's voice sounded far, far away.

"That's what happens sometimes with head injuries," the nurse replied.

Dr. Williams cancelled the plan to transfer her to a coma unit since it was clear Carey Spencer was waking up. Joe assigned another paramedic to cover his shift and stayed by her bedside, hoping to be there when she woke up again. The next time, hopefully, would be permanently. He had dozed off for a second.

"Where am I?" Her voice.

Had he slept a few minutes?

He forced open his eyes and faced Carey as she sat up in the bed, propped by several pillows. Her hair fell in a tangle of waves over her shoulders. Those dark green eyes flashed at him. She'd already figured out how to use the hand-held bed adjuster. "Where am I?" she asked more forcefully.

He'd told her earlier, but she'd suffered a head trauma, her brain was all jumbled up inside. Because of the concussion she might forget things for a long time to come. She deserved the facts.

"You're in the hospital in Hollywood, California. You got off a cross-country bus the other night. Do you remember where you came from?"

"I don't want anyone contacting my family."

He rang for the nurse. "We won't contact anyone unless you tell us to."

"I'm from Montclare, Illinois. It's on the outskirts of Chicago."

"Okay. Are you married?"

She shook her head, then looked at him tentatively. "I'm pregnant." Her eyes captured his and he could tell she remembered they'd gotten emotional together earlier when she'd woken up before. "And my baby's okay." She gave a gentle smile and odd protective sensations rippled over him. Those green eyes and the dark auburn hair. Wow. Her blackened eye may have been healing, but even with the shiner she was breathtaking. In his opinion anyway.

"Yes. Everything is okay in that department. How far along are you? Do you know?"

"Three months."

"And you came here on the bus for...?"

She hesitated. "Not for. To get away." She lifted her arms, covered in fading bruises. "I needed to get away."

"I understand." The uncompromising need to protect her welled up full force again. "Are you in trouble?"

She shook her head, then looked like it hurt to do so and immediately stopped.

The nurse came in, and asked Joe to leave so she could assess her patient and attend to her personal needs. He headed toward the door.

"Wait!" she said.

He turned.

"What's your name?"

"I'm Joseph Matthews. I'm the paramedic who brought you here."

"Thank you, Joseph. I owe you my life. And my baby's," she said from behind the privacy curtain.

He stared at his work boots, an uncertain smile creasing his lips. She certainly didn't owe him her life, but he was awfully glad to have been on scene the night she'd needed him.

The police were notified, and Joe didn't want to stick

around where he had no business, though in his heart he felt he deserved to know the whole story, so he went back to work. Around ten p.m., nearing the end of his shift, James approached. "Did you know she's a nurse?"

"I didn't. Interesting."

"She won't tell us how she got all banged up, but the fact she doesn't want us to contact the father of the baby explains that, doesn't it."

"Sadly, true."

"So, since she's recovering, if all goes well after tonight, I'm going to have to discharge her."

Startled by the news, Joe wondered why it hadn't occurred to him before. Of course she couldn't live here at the clinic. Her identity had been stolen along with her purse and any money she may have had in it. She was pregnant and alone in a strange city, and he couldn't very well let her become homeless, too. Hell, tomorrow was Sunday! "I've got an extra room. I could put her up until she gets back on her feet."

Joe almost did a second take, hearing himself make the offer, but when he thought more about it, he'd meant it. Every word. Even hoped she'd take him up on it.

"That's great," James said. "Though she may feel more comfortable staying with one of our nurses."

"True. Dumb idea, I guess."

"Not dumb. Pretty damn noble if you ask me. I'll vouch for you being a gentleman." James cast him a knowing smile and walked away.

Joe fought the urge to rush to Carey's room. She'd been through a lot today, waking up after a three-day sleep and all, and probably had a lot of thinking and sorting out to do. The social worker would be pestering her about her lost identification and credit cards and helping straighten out that mess. The poor woman's already bruised brain was probably spinning.

He needed to give her space, not make her worry he was some kind of weird stalker or something. But he wanted to tell her good night so he hiked over to the DOU and room Seventeen A, knocked on the wall outside the door, and when she told him to come in, he poked his head around the corner.

"Just wanted to say good night."

She seemed much less tense now and her smile came easily. She was so pretty, the smile nearly stopped him in his tracks. "Good night. Thanks for everything you've done for me."

"Glad to be of service, Carey."

"They're going to let me go tomorrow."

"Do you have a place to stay?"

"Not yet. Social Services is looking into something."

He walked closer to her bed and sat on the edge of his favorite chair. "I…uh… I have a two-bedroom house in West Hollywood. It's on a cul-de-sac, and it's really safe. Uh, the thing is, if you don't have any place to go, you can use my spare room. It's even got a private bathroom."

"You've done so much for me already. I couldn't—"

"Just until you get back on your feet. Uh, you know. If you want. That is." Why did he sound like a stammering, yammering teenager asking a girl on a date? That wasn't what he'd had in mind. He just wanted to help her. That was all.

She was the vision of a woman trying to make up her mind. Judging him on whether she could trust him or not, and from her recent experience Joe could understand why she might doubt herself. "Um, Dr. Rothsberg will vouch for me."

"I'll vouch for who?" James walked in on their awkward moment.

"I was just inviting Carey to stay in my spare room, if she needs a place to stay for a while."

James nailed Carey with his stare. "He's a good man. You can trust him." Then he turned and faced Joe and looked questioning. "I think."

That got a laugh out of Carey, and Joe shook his head. Guys loved to mess with each other.

"Okay, then," she said, surprising the heck out of Joe. "Okay?"

"Yes. Thank you." The woman truly knew how to be gracious, and for that he was grateful.

He smiled. "You're welcome. I'll see you tomorrow, then." It was his day off, but he'd be back here in a heartbeat when she was ready for discharge.

He turned to leave, unusually happy and suddenly finding the need to rush home and clean the house.

CHAPTER THREE

JOE HAD WORKED like a fiend to clean his house that morning before he went to the clinic to bring Carey back. He'd gotten her room prepared and put his best towels into the guest bathroom, wanting her to feel at home. He'd stocked the bathroom with everything he thought she might need from shampoo to gentle facial soap, scented body wash, and of course a toothbrush and toothpaste. Oh, and a brush for that beautiful auburn hair.

Aware that Carey only had the clothes on her back, he'd pegged her to be around his middle sister Lori's size and had borrowed a couple pairs of jeans and tops. Boy, he'd had a lot of explaining to do when he'd asked, too, since Lori was a typical nosy sister, especially since his divorce.

Once, while Carey had been sleeping in the clinic, he'd checked the size of her shoes and now he hoped she wouldn't mind that he'd bought her a pair of practical ladies' slip-on rubber-soled shoes and some flip-flops, because she couldn't exactly walk around in those sexy boots all the time. Plus, flip-flops were acceptable just about everywhere in Southern California. He was grateful some of the nurses had bought her a package of underwear and another bra—he'd heard that through the grapevine, thanks to Stephanie, the gossipy receptionist at The Hollywood Hills Clinic, who'd said she'd gone in on the collection of money for said items.

Now he waited in the foyer for the nurse or orderly to bring Carey around for discharge, having parked his car in the circular driveway. Careful not to say anything to Stephanie about the living arrangements, knowing that if he did so the whole clinic would soon find out, he smiled, assured her that Social Services had arranged for something, and with crossed arms tapped his fingers on his elbows, waiting.

She rounded the corner, being pushed in a wheelchair—clinic policy for discharges, regardless of how well the patient felt, but most especially for someone status post-head injury like her. She was dressed the way he'd first seen her last Wednesday night, and she trained her apprehensive glance straight at him. Even from this distance he noticed those dark green eyes, and right now they were filled with questions. Yeah, it would be weird to bring a strange lady into his home, especially one who continuously made his nerve endings and synapses react as if she waved some invisible magnetic wand.

He wanted to make her feel comfortable, so he smiled and walked to pick up the few things she had stuffed into a clinic tote bag, a classier version of the usual plastic discharge bags from other hospitals he'd worked at. It was one of the perks of choosing The Hollywood Hills Clinic for medical care, though in her case she hadn't had a choice.

It was nothing short of a pure leap of faith, going home with a complete stranger like this, Carey knew, but her options were nil and, well, the guy *had* cried with her that first day in the hospital when she'd woken up. The only thing that had mattered to her after the mugging was her baby, and when she'd been reassured it was all right, she'd been unable to hold back the tears. Joseph Matthews was either the easiest guy crier she'd ever met or the most empathetic man on the planet. Either way, it made him special. She had to remember that. Plus he'd saved her life. She'd *never* forget that.

When Dr. Rothsberg had vouched for him, and she'd already noticed how everyone around the clinic seemed to like the guy, she'd made a snap decision to take the paramedic up on his offer. But, really, where else did she have to go, a homeless shelter? She'd been out of touch with her parents for years and Ross was the reason she'd run away. She had zero intention of contacting any of them.

Recent history proved she couldn't necessarily trust her instincts, but she still had a good feeling about the paramedic.

When they first left the clinic parking lot Joseph slowed down so she could look back and up toward the hillside to the huge Hollywood sign. Somehow it didn't seem nearly as exciting as she'd thought it would be. Maybe because it hurt to turn her head. Or maybe because, being that close, it was just some big old white letters, with some parts in need of a paint touch-up. Now she sat in his car, her head aching, nerves jangled, driving down a street called Highland. Having passed the Hollywood Bowl and going into the thick of Hollywood, she admitted to feeling disappointed. Where was the magic? To her it was just another place with crowded streets in need of a thorough cleaning.

It was probably her lousy mood. She'd never planned on visiting California. She'd been perfectly happy in

Montclare. She'd loved her RN job, loved owning her car, being independent for the first time in her life. She still remembered the monumental day she'd gotten the key to her first apartment and had moved out once and for all from her parents' house. Life had been all she'd dreamed it would be, why would she ever need to go to Hollywood?

Then she'd met Ross Wilson and had thought she'd fallen in love, until she'd realized too late what kind of man he really was.

Nope. She'd come to Hollywood only because it had been the first bus destination she'd found out of Chicago. For her it hadn't been a matter of choice, but a matter of life and death.

Back at his house, Joe gave Carey space to do whatever she needed to do to make herself at home in her room. She'd been so quiet on the ride over, he was worried she was scared of him. He'd probably need to tread lightly until she got more comfortable around him. He thought about taking off for the afternoon, giving her time to herself, but, honestly, he worried she might bolt. Truth was, he didn't know what she might do, and his list of questions was getting longer and longer. All he really knew for sure was that he wanted to keep her safe.

The first thing he heard after she'd gone to her room had been the shower being turned on, and the image that planted in his head needed to be erased. Fast. So he decided to work out with his hanging punchbag in his screened-in patio, which he used as a makeshift gym. He changed clothes and headed to the back of the house, turned on a John Coltrane set, his favorite music to hit the bag with, and got down to working out.

With his hands up, chin tucked in, he first moved in

and out around the bag, utilizing his footwork, warming up, moving the bag, pushing it and dancing around, getting his balance. With bare hands he threw his first warm-up punches, *slap, slap, slap*, working the bag, punching more. The stitches across his rib cage pulled and stung a little, but probably wouldn't tear through his skin. Though after the first few punches he checked to make sure. They were healing and held the skin taut that was all.

As his session heated up, so did the wild saxophone music. He pulled off his T-shirt and got more intense, beating the hell out of the innocent bag where he mentally pasted every wrong the world had ever laid at his feet. His wife sleeping with his best friend, the lies about her baby being his. The divorce. He worked through the usual warm-up, heating up quickly. Then he pounded that bag for women abused by boyfriends and innocent victims who got mugged after getting off buses. *Wham*. He hit that bag over and over, pummeling it, his breath huffing, sweat flying. *Thump, bam, whump!*

"Excuse me, Joseph?"

Jolted, he halted in mid-punch, first stabilizing the punchbag so it wouldn't swing back and hit him, then shifted his gaze toward Carey. She had on different jeans, and one of his sister's bright pink cotton tops, and her wet hair was pulled up into a ponytail, giving her a wholesome look. Which he thought was sexy.

"Oh. Hey. Call me Joe. Everything okay?" he asked, out of breath.

"That music sounds like fighting." She had to raise her voice to be heard over the jazz.

"Oh, sorry, let me turn it off." That's why he liked

to work out with Coltrane, it got wild and crazy, often the way he felt.

Her gaze darted between his naked torso and his sweaty face. "I was just wondering if I could make a sandwich."

"Of course. Help yourself to anything. I've got cold cuts in the fridge. There's some fruit, too."

"Thanks." Her eyes stayed on his abdomen and he felt the need to suck it in, even though he didn't have a gut. "You know you're bleeding?"

He glanced down. Sure enough, he'd tugged a stitch too hard and torn a little portion of his skin. "Oh. Didn't realize." He grabbed his towel and blotted it quickly.

"Did you get hurt when you helped me?"

"Yeah, the jerk sliced me with his knife." Still blotting, he looked up.

Her eyes had gone wide. "You risked your life for me? I'm so sorry."

"Hey, I didn't risk my life." Had he? "I was just doing my job."

"Do paramedics usually fight guys with blades in their hands?"

"Well, maybe not every day, but it could happen." He flashed a sheepish grin over the bravado. "At least, it has now."

Her expression looked so sad he wanted to hug her, but they hardly knew each other.

"Thank you." He sensed she also meant she was sorry.

"Not a problem. Glad to do it." He waited to capture her eyes then nodded, wanting to make sure she understood she deserved nothing less than someone saving her from an alley attacker. They stood staring at each other for a moment or two too long, and since he was the one who always got caught up in the magic of her eyes, she looked away first. Standing in his boxing shorts, shirtless, he felt like he'd been caught naked winning that staring match.

"So... I'm going to make that sandwich." She pointed toward the door then led into the small kitchen, just around the corner from the dining area and his patio, while he assessed his stitches again. Yeah, he'd taken a knife for her, but the alternative, her getting stabbed by a sleazebag and maybe left to die, had been unacceptable.

The woman had a way of drumming up forgotten protective feelings and a whole lot more. Suddenly the house felt way too small for both of them. How was he going to deal with that while she stayed here?

Maybe one last punch to the bag then he promised to stop. *Thump!* The stitches tugged more and smarted. He hated feeling uncomfortable in his own house and blamed it on the size. He'd thought about selling it after Angela had agreed to leave, but the truth was he liked the neighborhood, it was close enough to work, and most of his family lived within a ten-mile radius. And why should he have to change his life completely because his wife had been unfaithful? Okay, one last one-two punch. *Whump, thump. Ouch, my side.* He grabbed his towel again and rubbed it over his wringing-wet hair.

One odd thought occurred to him as he dried himself off. When was the last time a woman had seen him shirtless? His ex-wife Angela had left a year ago, and was a new mother now. Good luck with that. He hadn't brought anyone home since she'd left, choosing to throw himself into his expanding business and demanding job rather than get involved with any poor unsuspecting women. He was angry at the world for being sterile, and angrier at the two people he'd trusted most, his wife and his best friend. Where was a guy supposed to go from there? Ah, what the hell. He punched the bag again. *Wham thud wham.*

"Would you like a sandwich?"

Not used to hearing a female voice in his house, it startled him from his down spiraling thoughts. A woman, a complete stranger no less, was going to be staying here for an indeterminate amount of time. Had he been crazy to offer? Two strangers in an eleven-hundred-square-foot house. That was too damn close, with hardly a way to avoid each other. Hell, their bedrooms were only separated by a narrow hallway and the bathrooms. What had he been thinking? His stomach growled. On the upside, she'd just offered to make him a sandwich.

Besides everything he was feeling—the awkwardness, the getting used to a stranger—he could only imagine she felt the same. Except for the unwanted attraction on his part, he was quite sure that wasn't an issue for her—considering her situation, she must feel a hell of a lot more vulnerable. He needed to be on his best behavior for Carey. She deserved no less.

"Yes, thanks, a sandwich sounds great." Since the bleeding had stopped, he tossed on his T-shirt after wiping his chest and underarms, then joined her in the kitchen.

"Do you like lettuce and tomato?"

"Whatever you're having is fine. I'm easy." His hands hung on to both sides of the towel around his neck.

"I never got morning sickness, like most women do. I've been ravenous from the beginning, so you're getting the works."

She was tallish and slender, without any sign of being

pregnant, and somehow he found it hard to believe she ate too much. "Sounds good. Hey, I thought I'd barbecue some chicken tonight. You up for that?"

She turned and shared a shy smile. "Like I said, I'm always hungry, so it sounds good to me."

He got stuck on the smile that delivered a mini sucker punch and didn't answer right away. "Okay. It looks like it'll be nice out, so I thought we could eat outdoors on the deck." He needed to put some space between them, and it wouldn't feel as close or intimate out there. *Just keep telling yourself she's wearing your sister's clothes. Your sister's clothes.*

He'd done a lot with his backyard, putting in a garden and lots of shrubbery for privacy's sake from his neighbors, plus he'd built his own cedar-plank deck and was proud of how it'd turned out. It had been one of the therapeutic projects he'd worked on during the divorce.

The houses had been built close together in this neighborhood back in the nineteen-forties. He liked to refer to it as his start-up house, had once planned to start his family in it, too. Too bad it had been someone else's family that had gotten started here.

Fortunately, Carey interrupted his negative thoughts again jabbing a plate with a sandwich into his side. He took the supremely well-stacked sandwich and grabbed some cold water from the refrigerator, raised the bottle to see if she'd like one. Without a word she nodded, and put her equally well-stacked sandwich on a second plate. As he walked to the dining table with the bottles in one hand and his sandwich in the other, he called out, "Chips are on the counter."

"Already found them," she said, appearing at the table, hands full with food and potato-chips bag, knocking him over the head with her smile—how much could a lonely man take? Obviously she was ready to eat.

It occurred to him they had some natural communication skills going on, and the thought made him uneasy. Beyond uneasy to downright uncomfortable. He clenched his jaw. He didn't want to communicate with a woman ever again. At least not yet, anyway, but since he'd just had a good workout and he was hungry, starved, in fact, he'd let his concerns slide. For now. Carey proved to be a woman of her word, too, matching him bite for bite. Yeah, she could put it away.

After they'd eaten, Carey asked to use his phone to make some calls.

"What'd I say earlier? *Mi casa es su casa.* It's a California rule. Make yourself at home, okay?" Though he said it, he wasn't anywhere near ready to meaning it.

"But it's long distance."

"I know you've got a lot of things to work out. All your important documents were stolen." This, helping her get her life back in order, he could do. The part of living with a woman again? Damn, it was hard. Sometimes, just catching the scent of her shampoo when she walked past seemed more than he could take.

"The clinic social worker has been helping me, and my credit cards have been cancelled now. But I couldn't even order new ones because I didn't have an address to send them to."

"You've got one now." He looked her in the eyes, didn't let her glance away. He'd made a promise to himself on her behalf that he'd watch over her, take care of her. It had to do with finding her completely helpless in that alley and the fierce sense of protectiveness he'd felt. "You can stay here as long as you need to. I'm serious."

She sent him a disbelieving look. In it Joe glimpsed

how deeply some creep back in Illinois had messed her up and it made him want to deck the faceless dude. But he also sensed something else behind her disbelief. "Thank you."

"Sure. You're welcome." Though she only whispered the reply, he knew without a doubt she was really grateful to be here, and that made the nearly constant awkward feelings about living with a complete stranger, a woman more appealing than he cared to admit, worth it.

Later, over dinner on the deck in the backyard, Joe sipped a beer and Carey lemonade. Her hair was down now, and she'd put on the sweater she'd worn that first night over his sister's top. In early June, the evenings were still cool, and many mornings were overcast with what they called "June gloom" in Southern California. She'd spent the entire dinner asking about his backyard and job, which were safe topics, so it was fine with him. Since she'd been asking so many questions, he got up the nerve to ask her one of the several questions he had for her. Also within the safe realm of topics—work.

"I heard at the clinic that you're a nurse?"

She looked surprised. "Yes. That was the call I made earlier, to the hospital where I worked. I guess you could say I'm now officially on a leave of absence."

"So you'll probably go back there when you feel better?" Why did this question, and her possible answer, make him feel both relief and dread? He clenched his jaw, something he'd started doing again since Carey had moved in.

She grimaced. "I can't. I'll have to quit at some point, but for now I'm using the sick leave and vacation time I've saved up and, I hope you don't mind, I gave them your address so they could mail my next check to me here."

"Remember. *Mi casa es tuya.*" He took another drag on his longneck, meaning every word in the entire extent of his Spanish speaking, but covering for the load of mixed-up feelings that kept dropping into his lap. What was it about this girl that made him feel so damn uncomfortable?

His practiced reply got a relieved smile out of her, and he allowed himself to enjoy how her eyes slanted upward whenever she did. It was dangerous to notice things like that and, really, what was the point? But having the beer had loosened him up and he snuck more looks than usual at her during dinner. "The clinic is always looking for good nurses. What's your specialty?"

"I work, or I should say worked, in a medical-surgical unit. I loved it, too."

"See..." he pointed her way "...that would fit right in. When you feel better, maybe you should look into it. I can talk to James about it if you'd like." *Yeah, keep these interactions all about helping her, and maybe she'll skip the part about asking you about yourself.*

"James?"

"Dr. Rothsberg."

"First I have to get my RN license reissued from Illinois since it was stolen along with everything else."

So maybe she did have plans to stay here and seek employment. Now he could get confused again and try to ignore that flicker of hope he'd kept feeling since she'd walked into his life. He ground his molars. "Would your license be accepted in California?"

"I did some research on the bus ride out and I'll have to apply here in California. That'll take some time, I suspect."

"Well, I'm working days tomorrow, so you can spend the whole day using my computer and phone and maybe start straightening out everything you need to."

She nodded. "I do have some people I owe a call." Deep in thought, she probably went straight to the gazillion things she'd have to do to re-create herself and begin a new life for her and her baby in a new state. He wouldn't want to be in her shoes, and wished he could somehow help even more. Would that go beyond his promise to watch over her?

At least the social worker and the police department had started the ball rolling on a few things. But, man, what a mess she had to clean up, especially since she hadn't wanted her family notified of her whereabouts. Why was that?

Joe wanted to ask her about her living situation back home, but suspected she'd shut down on him like a trapdoor if he did this soon, so he tucked those questions into his "bring up later" file. With an ironic inward laugh, he supposed they had a lot in common, not wanting to bring up the past and all. "You feel like watching a little TV?" He figured she could use something to distract her from all the things she'd have to tackle tomorrow.

"I'd like that but only after you let me clean up from dinner."

"Only if you'll let me help." Hell, could they get any more polite?

She smiled. "So after we do the dishes, what would you like to watch?"

"You choose." Yeah, he'd let his guest make all the decisions tonight. It was the right thing to do.

"I like that show about zombies."

"Seriously?" He never would have pegged her as a

horror fan. "It's my favorite, too, but I didn't think it would be good for your bambino."

"Ha," she said, picking up the dishes from the bench table on the outdoor deck. "After what this little one has been through already, a pretend TV show should be a walk in the park." She glanced down at her stomach while heading inside and toward the kitchen. "Isn't that right, sweetie pie."

There he went grinding his molars again. He followed her in and watched her put the dishes on the counter and unconsciously pat her abdomen then smile. That simple act sent a flurry of quick memories about Angela and how excited they'd once been when she'd first found out she'd gotten pregnant. They'd been about to give up trying since it had been over a year, had even had fertility tests done. They'd rationalized that because they were both paramedics and under a lot of stress, and he worked extended hours trying to make a good impression with Dr. Rothsberg, that was the reason she'd been unable to get pregnant.

So they'd taken a quickie vacation. Then one day, wham, she magically announced she was expecting. Joe had practically jumped over the moon that night, he'd been so happy. They'd finally start their own version of a big happy family. Since Angela's body had gotten the hang of getting pregnant, he'd planned to talk her into having a few more kids after this one. He'd walked on air for a couple of months...until his fertility report had dropped into the mailbox. Late. Very, very late.

What a fool he'd been.

Trying to give his overworked jaw a break, Joe went to town scrubbing the grill from the barbecue as if it was a matter of life and death. By the time they'd finished with the cleanup, he didn't know about Carey any more, but he definitely needed the distraction of some mindless TV viewing.

She sat on the small couch, passing him along the way, and he caught the scent of her shampoo again. It was a fresh, fruity summer kind of smell with a touch of coconut, which when he'd bought it for her had never planned for it to be a minor form of torture.

Mixed up about his feelings for the smart and easy-going nurse from Illinois, he intentionally sat on the chair opposite the couch, not ready to get too close to her again tonight. It brought up too many bad memories, and he so did not want to go there. There was only so much boxing a guy could do in a day. Torture sounded better than reliving his failed marriage. He clicked on the TV right on time for the show they both liked to escape to. If zombies couldn't make him forget how attracted he was to the lovely stranger living in his house, nothing could.

Carey put her head on the pillow of the surprisingly comfortable guest bed, thinking it was the first time she could remember feeling safe in ages. Things had gotten super-tense living with Ross those last few weeks, and, talk about the worst timing in the world, she'd gotten pregnant right around the time she'd known she had to leave him.

She didn't want to think about that now, because it would keep her awake, and she was really tired. It'd felt so normal and relaxing to sit and watch TV with Joe. He'd made the best barbecue chicken she'd ever eaten and she'd made a pig out of herself over the baked potato with all the toppings, but she chalked it up to his making her feel so welcome. The only problem was she couldn't get the vision of him in his boxing shorts, working out with the punchbag, out of her mind. Wow, his lean body had showcased every muscle in his arms and across his back as he'd punched. His movements had been fluid and nothing short of perfection. Not to mention his washboard stomach and powerful legs. The guy didn't have an ounce of fat on him.

What on earth was she thinking? Her life was in a shambles. She had an unborn baby to take care of. The last thing she should be thinking about was a man.

A naturally sexy man with kind brown eyes and a voice soothing enough to give her chills. She squeezed her eyes tight and shook her head on the pillow.

When she finally settled down and began to drift off to sleep she realized this was the first day she'd ever felt positive about her and the baby's future in three months. Things would work out for her, she just knew it. Because she, with the help of Joe, would make sure they did.

A slight smile crossed her lips as a curtain of sleep inched its way down until all was dark and she peacefully crossed into sweet dreams. Thanks to Joe.

CHAPTER FOUR

ON MONDAY, AFTER working all day, Joe insisted Carey come out with him for dinner, which was fine with her because she'd felt kind of cooped up. They ate at a little diner, then he showed her around Santa Monica, like the perfect host. She got the distinct impression it was to get them, and keep them, out of the house, because sometimes things felt too close there.

At least, that's how it felt for her, and sometimes she sensed it was the same for him. The guy seemed to bite down on his jaw a lot! But she soon ignored her worries about him not wanting her around and went straight to loving seeing the beach and the Pacific Ocean, and especially the Santa Monica pier.

On Tuesday Joe had the day off, and he dutifully took her shopping for more clothes at a place called the Beverly Center. They checked the directory and he guided her to the few stores she'd shown interest in, then he stood outside in the mall area, giving her space to shop. Clearly he wanted nothing to do with helping her choose clothes, rather he just did what he thought he should do out of courtesy to her situation. She protested all the way when he insisted on paying for everything. She sensed his generosity was based on some sense of charitable obligation, and she only accepted his offer when he'd agreed to let her repay him once she was back on her feet. She'd be sure to keep a tally because things were quickly adding up!

Wednesday morning, before he started an afternoon shift, he chauffeured her around to the Department of Motor Vehicles for a temporary driving license, and since she'd received a check from her old job he also helped her open a bank account. She decided the guy was totally committed to helping her, like he'd signed some paper or made some pact to do it. And she certainly appreciated everything he'd done for her, but...

Even though he was easy enough to be around, she felt it was out of total obligation to treat people right in life. Far too often she sensed a disconnect between his courtesy and that safe distance he insisted on keeping between them. Well, if that's what he wanted, she knew exactly how to live that way. Her parents had, sadly, been perfect role models in that regard.

Joe got home on Wednesday night to a quiet house. Carey had said hello, but now kept mostly to herself in her room. It made him wonder if he'd done something to offend her. He'd been trying his best to make her feel at home, though admittedly he may have been going about it robotically. But that seemed the only way he could deal with having a woman in his life again. Since he worked the a.m. shift the next day, he didn't get a chance to ask Carey if he'd put her off or if her withdrawal had nothing to do with him. Something was definitely on her mind, and under the circumstances, being battered, bruised, mugged, homeless, and completely vulnerable, not to mention living with a stranger, he could understand why.

Maybe he'd come off aloof or unapproachable at

times. But she had no idea how nearly unbearable it was to fix meals with her when it reminded him how much he missed being married. And having Carey there twenty-four seven, with her friendly smile and naturally sweet ways, was nearly making him come unhinged. She deserved someone to share things with, to talk to, but it couldn't be him. Nope. He was nowhere near ready or able to be her sounding board. All he'd signed up for was offering her a place to live.

Maybe he could arrange for some follow-up visits with the social worker at the clinic. That way she could get what she wanted and needed and he wouldn't have to be the person listening. Because when a woman vented, from his past experience with Angela, he knew she always expected something in return. Nope, no way would he unload his lousy past on Carey, no matter how much she might think she wanted him to. The lady had far too much on her plate as it was, and, truthfully, reliving such pain was the last thing he ever wanted to do. The social worker was definitely the right person to step in, and he planned to ask Helena to follow up the next day.

On Thursday evening, Joe came home to find Carey scrubbing the kitchen floor. From the looks of the rest of the house, she'd been cleaning all day.

"What's up?" he asked.

She was so focused on the floor-scrubbing she didn't notice him. He stepped closer but not onto the wet kitchen tiles.

"Am I that much of a slob?" he tried to joke, but she didn't laugh. Something was definitely eating at her. "Carey?"

Finally she heard him and shook her head as if she'd

been in a trance and looked at him. "Hi." Not sounding the least bit enthusiastic.

"Everything okay?"

She stopped pushing the mop handle. "Just trying to pay you back for all you're doing for me."

Damn. She may as well have sliced him with a knife. "You don't have to be my house cleaner, you know."

"What else can I do?" The obvious "else" *not* being to sleep together.

Why was that the first thought to come to his mind? Cripes, she had him mixed up. He used her clear frustration as a springboard to what his latest mission on Carey's behalf had been. "I, uh, spoke to the social worker today—the one who helped you while you were in the hospital—and she said she'd love to keep in touch." He'd totally reworded their true conversation, trying to make it sound casual, not necessary, but the truth was he'd talked at great length with Helena at work about Carey's precarious situation. The social worker wanted to keep connected with Carey and promised to call her right away.

"Yes. Thanks. She called earlier today. I'm going to have a phone appointment with her on Monday."

"That's great." He almost said, *I hope it helps you snap out of your funk,* but kept that thought to himself because a sneaky part of him worried he'd put her there. He knew too well how unhelpful being told to snap out of it could be, especially when a person was nowhere near ready. He would protect Carey in any way he could, and felt she shouldn't be nervous all the time. But he'd never been in her shoes, and…

Then it dawned on him. Why hadn't he thought of it before? The woman was a nurse. Nurses were always busy on the job. She was used to helping people, not the other way around. She was probably going crazy with so much time on her hands and nothing to do but watch TV or read while he was away every day. But she'd had a head trauma and needed to heal. "Do you feel ready to go back to work?"

She shifted from being intent on cleaning to suddenly looking deflated. "That's the thing, I can't until the California RN license comes through. Plus I still feel foggy-headed from the concussion. At this point I'd worry I might hurt some poor unsuspecting patient or something. But on another level my energy is coming back, and I'm feeling really restless."

That damn mugger had not only stolen her identity and money but also her confidence. He thought quickly. It was early summer, people went on vacations. "I think there might be some temporary slots to fill in while people go on vacation. Jobs that don't require a nursing license."

She stopped mopping and looked at him, definite interest in her eyes.

"For instance, I know of a ward clerk on the second floor who's getting ready to visit her family back east for two weeks. Maybe you could fill in on something like that. Sort of keep your hand in medicine but in a safer position until you feel back to your old self."

She rested her chin on the mop handle. "How can I just walk in off the street and expect to get a job in a hospital like The Hollywood Hills Clinic?"

He flashed an overconfident grin he hadn't used in a long time. "By knowing a guy like me? I could put in a good word to Dr. Rothsberg for you. What do you say?"

The fingers of one hand flew to her mouth as she thought. "That would be great. But it would also mean

I'd have to quit my job back home." Worry returned to her brow.

Joe was sure he was missing out on another story, probably something huge. Like, who she was running away from, and would they come after her? If only he could get her to open up. This was stuff he needed to know if he expected to protect her. Rather than press her right then, he let her finish her task and went to his room. Besides, he needed time to figure things out for himself, like the fact that he both totally looked forward to seeing her each day but dreaded how it made him feel afterwards.

After he changed into workout clothes, he headed to the back porch for some boxing, since it was the one sure way to help him blow off steam. Well into his usual routine, while she was in the other room, watching TV, he wondered if, in fact, the guy who'd given Carey her shiner might come after her, and an idea popped into his head. "Hey, Carey, come out here a minute, would you?"

Within seconds she showed up looking perplexed, and maybe like she'd rather be watching TV. Yeah, she'd probably already had it with living with him.

"Since you were mugged recently, and I'm sure you never want to go through that again, would you like me to show you a couple of moves?"

She looked hesitant, like learning a few self-defense maneuvers might bring back too many bad memories.

"Maybe it's too soon," he quickly.

"No, I can't keep hiding out at your house. I know there's a bus stop right down at the end of your street, and I shouldn't be afraid to use it." She nodded, a flicker of fight in her eyes. "Yeah, show me how I could have kept that creep from dragging me into the alley that night."

"That's the attitude," Joe said with a victorious smile. She smiled back, that spirited flash intensifying.

"Okay." He clapped his hands once. "I saw the guy grab you by the wrist and pull you away that night. So, first off, a lot of the information that's on the internet for ladies' self-defense is bogus. Here's something that works. When that guy grabbed your wrist, you could have used your other hand to push into his eyes, or, if he wore glasses, you could have gone for his throat. With either move you also could have included a knee to the groin. That stuff hurts the attacker and surprises them. Knocks them off balance. Let me show you."

He grabbed Carey's right wrist and immediately felt her tense, making him think maybe he was right and it was too early to do this lesson with her. But he was committed now and pressed on, and she had enough anger in her eyes to put it to good use.

"Okay, use your left hand and go for my face," He showed her how to make an open, claw-like spread with the fingers and how to jab it at a person's face to do the most damage. "Get those fingers on my eyes and press with all your might."

She followed his instructions and went for his eyes.

"Ow!" He reacted and pushed her hand back to keep her from injuring him.

"Sorry!"

"Don't be sorry, fight for your life. It's up to me to keep you from hurting me. You just caught me off guard. Got it?"

She gave one firm and committed nod.

"That's the spirit. If the guy foils that move with his other hand, like I just did, make sure you put your knee to his groin at the same time." He flashed a charming grin. "Don't actually do that one now, okay?"

She laughed, and it felt good to get her to relax a little.

"Just knee him in the groin area and later you can practice kneeing the heck out of that boxing bag."

"Got it, boss." Yes, she was really into this now.

He said, "Go!" and grabbed her left wrist this time, and she moved like lightning for his face and eyes, driving her knee into his groin at the same time. Being prepared for the move, in case she got overzealous, which she obviously had, he brought his own knee up and across to protect himself, letting her full force hit his thigh. If he hadn't, he'd have been on his hands and knees, riding out the pain, right now.

He didn't want to discourage her efforts but, damn, that could have hurt! "Good." Up close, their eyes locked. He could hear her breathing hard and felt the pulse in her wrist quicken. The fire in her green-eyed stare made him take notice. He stepped back, releasing her wrist. "That was good."

She rubbed her wrist and searched the floor with her gaze, making a quick recovery. This wasn't easy to relive, he understood that, but keeping the same thing from ever happening again was more important than her current comfort zone.

"Now do the same thing, going for my throat." He showed her the wide V of his hand between the thumb and index finger and demonstrated how to drive it into the Adam's apple area of the attacker's neck. "Since most guys, like that scumbag the other night, will be taller than you, force your hand upward with all you've got. Okay?"

Carey agreed and he immediately grabbed her hand, trying to catch her off guard. Something clicked, like she'd gone back in time. She went into attack mode and because he wasn't ready for it she got him good in the throat. He coughed and sputtered and backed away to recover, and only then did she realize she'd shifted from demonstration to true life.

"I'm sorry!" she squealed, grabbing her face with her hands, as if just snapping out of a bad dream.

He swallowed, trying to get his voice back. "That's the way. See how it works? I dropped your hand, and that means you could have run off screaming for help at that point."

"Oh, Joe." Carey rushed to him. "I'm so sorry I hurt you." She touched his shoulder and, without thinking, he reacted by opening his arms. Carey threw her arms around him and squeezed. "Can I get you some water? Anything?"

"Maybe a new throat," he teased, though he really liked having her arms around him, the realization nearly making him lose his balance. She smelled a hell of a lot better than he did, and up close, like this, her eyes were by far the prettiest he'd ever seen in his life, though fear seemed to have the best of them right now.

Surprised, no, more like stunned by how moved she'd been when grappling with Joe, Carey held him perhaps a second too long. Fear still pounded in her chest. At first the lesson had brought out all the bad memories she'd been trying to force down a few months before leaving home and definitely since coming to Hollywood. Ross had changed from attentive boyfriend to jealous predator. He had frightened her. He'd also grabbed her by the wrist like that on several occasions, each time scaring her into submission. Then the creep at the bus station must have seen her as an easy mark, sensed her fear, and grabbed her the same way, pulling her into the alley.

She hated feeling like a victim!

Anger had erupted as horrible memories had collided with Joe's grip on her wrist. She'd never be a victim again, damn it. Never. Suddenly fighting for her life all over again, she'd switched to kill mode and had practically pushed his larynx out the back of his neck. Darn it! She hadn't meant to hurt him, not the man who'd saved her and taken her in, but she clearly had.

Now, being skin to skin with her incredibly fit and appealing roommate had changed the topic foremost in her mind. Being in Joe's arms wiped out her fear and she shifted from fighting for her life to being completely turned on. What was it about Joe?

So confusing. It wasn't right.

Obviously her concussion was still messing with her judgment.

In a moment of clarity she broke away and strode to the kitchen to get him a glass of water, trying to recover before she brought it to him.

"What about pepper spray?" She schooled her voice to sound casual, completely avoiding his eyes, as if she hadn't just survived a flashback and had flung herself into Joe's arms. There was nothing wrong with a decoy topic to throw him off the scent, right? The man had turned her on simply by touching her. Pitiful. Blame it on the head injury.

"First you have to get it out of your purse, right?"

She nodded, quickly realizing the fault in her premise. He stood shirtless, damp from his workout, skin shiny and all his muscles on display. Cut and ripped. A work of art. She handed him the glass. Thought about handing him his T-shirt so he'd cover up and make her life a little safer for the moment, or less tempting anyway. At least it seemed easier for him to swallow now and that made her grateful she hadn't caused any permanent damage. Could she have? If so, he'd just given her a huge gift of self-protection. No way would she let herself be a victim. By God, she'd never let anyone hurt her again.

"Plus, I've heard about guys who've been sprayed and didn't even react," he continued. "Also, when you're scared or nervous, you might spray all over the place and not hit the eyes."

She kept nodding, watching him, completely distracted by his physique, unable to really listen, wishing she'd brought herself a cool drink too. Surely her head injury had left her brain unbalanced, taking her back to the worst moments in her life one second and then the next rushing into the realm of all things sensual.

"Your hands and your knees are your best defense. Want to practice again?"

She sucked in a breath and shook her head quickly. This was all too confusing. "I think that's enough for tonight."

He put down his glass on the nearby table, folded an arm across his middle, rested the other elbow on it and held his chin with his thumb and bent fingers, biting his lower lip and nailing her with a sexy, playful gaze. "Chicken, eh?"

Joe had saved her life. He'd also just given her a great gift of learning self-defense. And there *was* that sexy sparkle in his eyes right now...

"Are you challenging me?" Suddenly awash with tiny prickles of excitement again, she moved toward him and grabbed his wrist with all her might. "Let's see you fight your way out of this one, buddy." She knew she didn't have a chance in hell of keeping hold but enjoyed the moment, and especially grappling with the hunk. When was the last time she'd had fun horsing around with a man and not felt the least bit afraid or vulnerable?

She trusted Joe not to hurt her.

He swung his free arm around behind her and pulled her close, pretending to get her in a head lock but quickly moving into a backward hug. "I don't suggest you ever let your attacker get you in this position," he said playfully over the shell of her ear.

"There won't be any more attackers," she said through gritted teeth. "Because I'll kick their asses first."

He tightened his hold, but in a good way, a sexy way. She went limp in his arms, feeling his closeness in every cell and nerve ending, confused by the total attraction she had for him. This was the worst time in the world to fall for someone. She was pregnant with another man's baby, for crying out loud. He must have felt the shift of her mood from fight to flight, or in this case to catatonic, and he quickly backed off. They'd gotten too close. Too soon. That sexy, challenging gaze in his eyes from a second before disappeared and he reached for his water to take another drink as a distraction.

"So," he started again, sounding nonchalant, "another good idea, if a bad guy only wants your wallet, is to reach into your purse, grab your wallet and throw it as far away as you can. He probably wants your money, not you, and will go after it. Then scream like hell and run for your life. Of course, if he has a gun you may want to reconsider that move."

She gave the required light laugh over his obvious smart-aleck attempt to change the focus of what had just gone down. But their eyes met again, his honey brown and inviting as all hell, and it seemed they both knew some line had just been crossed. Though she couldn't tell from Joe's steely stare how he felt, and wasn't about to guess because the thought made her get all jittery inside, she hoped he couldn't tell how shaken she was.

She watched him with a mixture of shame and longing, but mostly confusion. Damn that concussion. "Thanks for the lesson," she whispered. "I'd better get some rest now."

They'd gotten too close, that was a fact.

She turned to head for her room, but a sense of duty stopped her. The man had saved her life then offered to share his home with her. Where did a guy like that come from? The least she could do was tell him what she'd been through, why she'd run away from home. He deserved to know how she'd ended up smack in the middle of his life. And if she shared, maybe she'd find out something about him, too.

"Joe?" She circled back to face him.

"Yeah?" He'd gone back to throwing punches at his punchbag and stopped.

"I ran away from a man who wanted to possess me. Completely. Little by little he clipped away at my life. Half the time I didn't even notice, until one day I realized he'd isolated me from everything I liked and loved other than him." She picked at a broken fingernail. "He wanted to control my life, and when I got pregnant he acted like that would ruin everything and got abusive with me." Carey stared at her feet rather than risk seeing any judgment on Joe's face. "I ran away the night he handed me a wad of money and told me to take care of 'it', as if my baby was a problem that needed fixing. He didn't want to share me with anyone, not even our kid."

She finally glanced up to find nothing but empathy in Joe's eyes. "I fought him and he roughed me up. So when he gave me the money I grabbed whatever I could without being obvious, acted like I was going to do what he wanted, then ran for my life."

Joe stepped toward her but she backed up, needing the distance and to tell him her entire story.

"I came to California because it was the next bus out of Montclare, and I didn't have time to pick or choose. I must have looked like a sitting duck because I stepped off the bus and immediately got dragged into that alley." Frightened to relive that night, and frustrated by the emotion rolling through her, she dug her fingers into her hair. "At first I thought maybe Ross had somehow found me and he was taking me back home. Then I realized I was getting mugged, but it was too late. I didn't know how to protect myself." She removed her hands from her hair and held them waist high, palms upward, beseeching Joe to understand. "If it wasn't for you I don't know where I'd be.

"I owe my life to you, and I've got to be honest and say it's strange to feel that way." She sat on the edge of the nearby dining table chair. "Yet here you are day after day watching over me, making my life better. I'm grateful, I am, but please understand that I'm confused and scared and..." Her voice broke with the words. "And I don't know what the future holds for me. Whether I stay here or go somewhere else, I just don't know, but the only thing that matters right now is my baby." Her forearm folded across her stomach and she blinked.

"I get it," Joe said. "Believe me, I understand how life-changing a baby can be."

"You do? Are you a father?"

"Uh, no." He immediately withdrew.

"So how do you know, then?"

"Look, forget I said that. Right now, all I want is for you to be healthy and safe." He came to her and crouched to be eye level with her. "I'm sorry if I've made you uncomfortable. I can't help but find you attractive, so there, I've said it, and I know that's not acceptable."

How was she supposed to answer him? "It may not be acceptable but I feel the same way." Oh, God, she'd put her secret thoughts into words. "It's just the worst timing in the world, you know?"

"I know. Like I said, I get it." He made the wise decision not to touch her but instead to stand and step back.

"Thank you for understanding."

"Of course."

She stood and started walking, this time without looking back, and headed on wobbly legs to her room. Had she just admitted she found Joe Matthews as attractive as he'd just confirmed he found her?

This was nuts! So she'd blame it on the head trauma.

Joe stood perfectly still, watching Carey make her exit. He half expected to hear her lock the door to the bedroom. He hoped he hadn't made her feel creepy about him. It hadn't been his intention to get her in a hug, but he'd been showing her ways to get out of predatory attacks and had inadvertently become a predator himself.

Great going, Joe. You made your house guest think you wanted to crawl into her bed.

He went back to the porch and punched the bag. "Ouch!" He hadn't prepared his fist and it hurt like hell. And what had gotten into him to let slip that he'd known how it felt to be an expectant parent? That wouldn't happen again. He wound up, wanting to punch the bag again, this time even harder, but stopped himself.

Regardless of how awkward he may have made Carey feel, she'd just opened up to him. Man, she'd had it tough back in Chicago. He couldn't remember the name of the suburb she'd come from, and right now that didn't matter. What mattered was that she shouldn't feel like she'd run all the way across country only to find herself in the same situation again.

She needed to get out of the house. To begin something. To get that job and start some money rolling in before she got so pregnant she wouldn't be able to. His head started spinning with everything that needed to be done for her. He needed to help her get her independence back.

From personal experience he knew about a special class at The Hollywood Hills Clinic. A class that would be perfect for where she was right now in her life. He knew the right people to talk to about it, too. And he'd move ahead with her getting that job, so if she wanted, in time, she could move out.

Maybe he couldn't erase what had happened between them just now, but he sure as hell could make some changes for the better happen, starting tomorrow.

He flipped off the light and headed to his room to take a cold shower and hopefully catch a little sleep.

On Friday afternoon Carey sat on the backyard deck in the shade of the huge jacaranda tree, the flowers falling into piles of light purple and scattering across the wood planks like pressed flowers in a painting. She'd been reading an article about early pregnancy on the internet on Joe's tablet when she heard his hybrid SUV pull into the garage and shortly after he came through the gate in the backyard.

Did he know she was out here? Or, more likely after last night, maybe he wanted to avoid her by coming through the back way, hoping she'd be inside.

"Hey," he said, all smiles, as if nothing monumental had occurred between them last night.

"Hi. You're home early."

He came toward the deck but didn't come up, keeping a safe distance between them, placing a foot on the second step and leaning a forearm over his knee. "One of the perks of owning your own business is that I call the shots. It was a slow day, so I took off early."

"Lucky you." His smile was wide, giving her the impression he had some good news. Maybe he had found somewhere for her to move to? If she was honest, that would give her mixed feelings, though the social worker Helena had said she'd look into housing for her, too, and she'd agreed to it at the time. "But I know you've worked hard to get where you are and at the ripe old age of twenty-eight you deserve your afternoon off. Twenty-eight, that's right isn't it?"

He nodded proudly. Yeah, he'd made something out of himself and he wasn't even thirty yet. "And you are?"

"Twenty-five."

"A mere child." He smiled, pretending to be the worldly-wise older man, but his gaze quickly danced away from hers. Yeah, he was still mixed up about last night, too. "So, listen, about you feeling isolated and stuck here and everything…"

"I didn't say that."

"You didn't have to. I figured it out after you went to your room last night. But let's not rehash that, because I've got some good news."

She shut down the tablet and leaned forward in the outdoor lounger. "Good news? They found my stuff?"

He wrinkled his nose and shook his head. "Sorry, I wish. But here's the deal—the clinic has this prenatal class, they call it Parentcraft and it's starting a new session tomorrow. I hope you don't mind, but I put your name in, and Dr. Rothsberg gave me the okay. I thought you could ride into work with me in the morning, and check it out."

"You signed me up? Isn't there a fee? I…uh…can't—"

"Like I said, James took care of everything. He's a generous man. There's a spot for you and the first session starts tomorrow at ten."

"Joe, I'm really grateful for you doing this, but you're helping so much, I don't think I'll ever be able to repay you."

"Carey, I'm not doing any of this to make you feel indebted to me. Please, don't feel that way. My parents taught me a lot of stuff, and helping folks was big in our family. When you're back on your feet you'll find a way to help someone else in need. That's all. No debt to me, just pay it forward."

"Joe…" She stared at him, trying her hardest to figure him out. Was he a freak of nature or her personal knight in shining armor? She leaned back in the lounger and looked into the blue sky dotted with its few wispy clouds. "It's just hard to take in all this goodness after the way my life had been going this past year." She heard him step up the stairs and walk toward her.

"Well, get used to it." He sat on the adjacent lounger then reached out to touch her hand. "That man you ran away from is ancient history. It may not have been your plan, but Hollywood is your new beginning. Just go with the flow, as my yoga-brained sister likes to say."

Carey laughed, wondering about Joe's family. They must be some special people to produce a gem like him. "Okay. Thanks. I'm excited about the class tomorrow."

"Great, and while you're at the hospital you can fill out the papers for the temporary ward clerk job, too."

"What?"

"I know, too much goodness, right?" He laughed, and she thought she could easily get used to watching his handsome face. "James, uh, Dr. Rothsberg, has taken care of everything. Hey, not every clinic can boast their very own Jane Doe. We just want to help get you back on your feet."

"This is all too much to take in."

"Then don't waste your time." He stood. "Come on, I'll take you to my favorite deli on Fairfax. You like roast beef on rye? They make their sandwiches this thick." He used his thumb and index finger to measure a good four inches.

Well, come to think of it, she was hungry. Again! And what better way to keep her mind off the whirl-wind of feelings gathering inside her about that man than stuffing her face with a sandwich. Otherwise she'd have to deal with her growing awareness of Joe, the prince of a guy who had literally come out of nowhere, protecting her, saving her, taking her in, changing her life in a positive way, and, maybe the most interesting part, forcing her to remember pure and simple attraction for the opposite sex.

Saturday morning Carey was up and dressed in one of the new outfits Joe had bought her, a simple summer dress with a lightweight pastel-green sweater that covered the tiny baby bump just starting to appear. She was nervous about applying for a job, though she knew she really needed to get out among the living again, to prove to herself she was getting back on her feet. Also, having something to do after a week of lying low since being discharged from the clinic was a major reason she looked forward to applying for the job. As for the parenting class, with her huge desire to be a good mother she was eager to start.

Joe had dressed for work, his light blue polo shirt with The Hollywood Hills Clinic logo above the pocket fit his healthy frame perfectly and highlighted those gorgeous deltoids, biceps and triceps. The cargo pants, though loose and loaded with useful pockets, filled with EMS stuff no doubt, still managed to showcase his fine derriere. She felt a little guilty checking him out as he walked ahead to open the door to the employee entrance. How much longer would she be able to blame her concussion for this irrational behavior? In her defense, there was just something so masculine about a guy wearing those serious-as-hell EMS boots!

He glanced at his watch. "You should have enough time to get your paperwork done for the job application first. I'll walk you over to HR."

"HR?"

"Human Resources."

"Ah, we call it Employee Relations back home."

"Yeah, same thing, but first I'm going to show you where your parenting class will be so you'll know where to go when you're through. Follow me."

Carey did as she was told, clutching her small purse with her new identification cards and temporary driving license, while walking and looking around the exquisite halls and corridors with vague memories of having been there before. Though the place seemed more like a high-end hotel than a hospital. And this time she had money from her last pay check from the hospital back home, instead of being completely vulnerable, like before. Ten days ago she'd arrived on a stretcher, and today she was applying for a job and starting a new parenting class. She was definitely getting back on her feet. Who said life wasn't filled with miracles?

"Oh, Gabriella," Joe said, to a pretty woman walking past, "I'd like to introduce you to Carey Spencer. She'll be starting your class later." He turned to Carey. "Gabriella is the head midwife and runs the prenatal classes."

The woman, who looked to be around Joe's age, with strawberry-blonde hair and a slim and healthy figure, smiled at Carey, her light brown eyes sparkling when she did so. They briefly shook hands, then all continued walking together, as the midwife was obviously heading somewhere in the same direction. As Gabriella was just about Carey's height, their eyes met when she spoke. "Oh, lovely to have you. How far along are you?"

"A little over three months."

"Perfect. We're beginning the class with pregnancy meal planning trimester by trimester, plus exercises for early pregnancy."

This was exactly what Carey needed. Just because she was a nurse it didn't mean she knew squat about becoming a mother or going through a pregnancy. "Sounds great." Her hopes soared with the lucky direction her life had taken. Thanks to Joe and Dr. Rothsberg.

"Yes, I think you'll love it." Gabriella cut off into another hallway. "Be sure to bring your partner," she said over her shoulder. "It's always good to have that reinforcement."

And Carey's heart dropped to her stomach, pulling her pulse down with it. Was having a partner a requirement? Obviously, Gabriella didn't know her circumstances.

Joe gave her an anxious glance. "That won't be a problem. Trust me, okay?"

Surely, Carey hoped, in this day and age there were

bound to be other women in the class without partners. Joe was probably right about it not being a problem. But, please, God, she wouldn't be the only one, would she?

Forty-five minutes later, after submitting her job application for the temporary third-floor medical/surgical ward clerk in HR and feeling very positive about it, Carey had found her way back to the modern and pristine classroom and took a seat. Several handouts had been placed on the tables. A dozen couples were already there, and more drifted in as the minutes ticked on. She glanced around the room, seeing a sea of couples. Oh, no, she really was going to be the only one on her own. How awkward would that be?

Fighting off feeling overwhelmed but refusing to be embarrassed, she glanced at the clock on the wall—three minutes to ten—and thought about sneaking out before the class began. She could learn this stuff online, and wouldn't have to come here feeling the odd man out every week. But Joe had gone out of his way to get her enrolled, and Dr. Rothsberg was footing the bill. She went back and forth in her mind about staying or going, then Gabriella entered and started her welcome speech.

She'd sat close to the back of the room, and it would still be easy to sneak out if she wanted or needed to. But, wait, she wasn't that person anymore, the one who let life throw her a curveball and immediately fell down. Nope, she'd turned in her victim badge, and Joe had helped her. She could do this. She forced her focus on the front of the class to Gabriella, who smiled and brightened the room with her lovely personality. The last thing Carey wanted to do was insult anyone, especially after Joe and Dr. Rothsberg had made special arrangements to get her here. But, oh, she felt weird about being the only single mom in the class.

"Why don't we go around the room and introduce ourselves?" Gabriella said.

Soon everyone else would notice, too.

The door at the back of the class opened again. Feeling nervous and easily distracted, Carey glanced over her shoulder then did a double take. In came Joe, his heavy booted steps drawing attention from several people in the vicinity.

"Sorry I'm late," he said to Gabriella, then walked directly to Carey and took the empty chair next to her. "If you don't mind," he whispered close to her ear, "I'll pretend to be your partner today." For all anyone else knew in the class, he could have told her he loved her. The guy knew how to be discreet, and from the way her heart pattered from his entrance he may as well have just run down a list of sweet nothings.

He'd obviously picked up on her anxiety the instant Gabriella had told her back in that hallway to be sure to bring her partner. He was here solely to spare her feelings.

Joseph Matthews truly was a knight in shining armor! Or in his case cargo pants and work boots.

As he settled in next to her his larger-than-life maleness quickly filled up the space between them. Warmth suffused her entire body. Being this close to Joe, having access to gaze into those rich brown eyes, would definitely make it difficult to concentrate on today's lesson.

"You're next, Carey. Introduce yourself and your partner," Gabriella said, emphasizing the *partner* part.

Joe hadn't meant to put Carey on the spot, but after seeing the panic in her eyes earlier, when Gabriella had told her to be sure to bring her partner, he couldn't let her go through this alone. At first he'd wanted to run like hell when he'd shown her the classroom. Coming here had brought back more awful memories. He and Angela had actually started this class before she'd moved out.

Feeling uneasy as hell when he'd dropped Carey off earlier, he'd gone back to his work station, but had soon found he'd been unable to concentrate on the job. His mind had kept drifting to Carey sitting here alone, feeling completely out of place, and he couldn't stand for that to happen. Besides, wasn't it time for him to move on? Determined to put his bad memories aside once and for all—his divorce hadn't been his fault—he'd made a decision. She shouldn't have to attend this class alone. If offering her support could ease her discomfort, he'd take the bullet for her and be her partner. The woman had been through enough on her own lately.

"Oh," she said, as if she'd never expected to have to introduce herself, even though everyone else just had. "Um, I'm Carey Spencer, I'm a little over three months pregnant, I, uh, recently moved to California." She swallowed nervously around the stretching of the truth. Joe reached for her hand beneath the table and squeezed it to give her confidence a boost. "I'm a nurse by profession, a first-time mother, and…" She looked at Joe, the earlier panic returning to those shimmering green eyes. He squeezed her hand again.

"I'm Joe Matthews," he stepped in. "Carey's friend. *Good* friend." He glanced at her, seeing her squirm, letting it rub off on him a tiny bit. "A really close friend." Overkill? He gazed around the room, having fudged the situation somewhat, and all the other couples watched expectantly. "We've been through a lot together, and we're both really looking forward to taking this class and learning how to be good parents."

Okay, let them think whatever they wanted. His

statement was mostly true—in fact, it was ninety-nine per cent true, except for the bit about being "really close" friends, though they had been through a lot together already. Oh, and the part about him ever getting to be a parent. Yeah, that would never happen. The reality hit like a sucker punch and he nearly winced with pain. Why the hell had he willingly walked into this room again? Carey's cool, thin fingers clasped his hand beneath the table, just as he'd done to support her a few seconds ago. The gesture helped him past the stutter in thought.

He'd come here today for Carey. She needed to catch a break, and he'd promised the night he'd found her in the alley that he'd look out for her. If she needed a partner for the parenting class then, damn it, he'd be here.

"I'm a paramedic here at the clinic, so if I ever need to deliver a baby on a run, I figure this class will be good for that, too." He got the laugh he was hoping for to relieve his mounting tension as the room reacted. "It's a win-win situation, right?"

He shifted his eyes to the woman to his left. If taking this class together meant having to really open up about themselves, well, he was bound to let her down because he was far, far from ready to talk about it.

Carey didn't know squat about his past, and if he had his way, she never would. Why humiliate himself again, this time in front of a woman he was quickly growing attached to, when once had already been enough for a lifetime?

CHAPTER FIVE

On the Saturday after the next Parentcraft class, Carey stood in the kitchen, using her second-trimester menu planner for dinner preparation. She'd had to stretch her usual eating routine to include items she'd never have been caught dead eating before. Like anchovies! Why was Gabriella so big on anchovies? Obviously they were high in calcium and other important minerals, plus loaded with omega three and six fatty acids, but Carey didn't think they tasted so great and smelled really bad. Carey practically had to hold her nose to eat them.

Fortunately this Saturday-night menu included salmon—yay, more omega fats—which Joe was dutifully grilling outside on a cedar plank. Dutiful, yeah, that was the right word for Joe. Everything he did for her seemed to be done out of duty. Sure, he was nice and considerate, but she never sensed he was completely relaxed around her.

She diligently steamed the broccoli and zucchini, and in another pot boiled some new red potatoes, grateful that Joe seemed okay to eat whatever she did. So far she'd managed to keep her occasional junk-food binges to herself. Nothing major, just items that had definitely been left off the Gabriella-approved dietary plan for a pregnant lady, like sea salt and malt vinegar potato chips, or blue corn chips, or, well, actually, any kind of chip that she could get her hands on. She rationalized that if occasionally she only bought the small luncheon-sized bags she wouldn't do the baby any harm. Or her hips.

Her weight gain was right on target, and when she'd seen Gabriella in clinic for a prenatal checkup, thanks to Dr. Rothsberg, she'd complimented her on how well she was carrying the baby. The ultrasound had been the most beautiful thing she'd ever seen, and the first person she'd wanted to share it with had been Joe, and since he'd brought her to the appointment, once she'd dressed she'd invited him back into the examination room. He'd oohed and aahed right along with her, but she'd sensed a part of him had remained safely detached. She could understand why—he was a guy and it wasn't his baby.

It made sense…yet he'd gotten all watery-eyed that day in the clinic when she'd found out her baby was okay, and he'd made that remark that one time about knowing how life-changing a baby could be. She'd asked him point blank if he was a father, but he'd said no and had powered right on. What had that been about? Heck, she'd only just recently found out how old he was, and the only thing she knew beyond that, besides he had a big, kind family, was that he was divorced.

The thing that kept eating away at her thoughts was that Joe didn't seem like the kind of guy who'd give up on a marriage.

Carey popped the top from another beer can and carried it outside to Joe. Being so involved together in the parenting class had definitely changed their relationship for the better, yet she knew Joe held back. She'd opened up about Ross in the hope of getting Joe to share whatever it was that kept him frequently tense and withdrawn.

At first she'd written off that always-present slow simmer just beneath the surface as being due to his demanding job as a paramedic, and also the fact he ran the business. But he clearly thrived on being in charge. It was obvious he loved the challenge. No, that wasn't the problem, it was when they were in the house together, her occasionally indulging in baby talk to her stomach, or discussing the latest information from the Parentcraft classes that she noticed him mentally slip into another time and place. Granted, another person's pregnancy wasn't exactly riveting to the average person, but Joe had volunteered to attend the class with her. If it was an issue, why had he signed on?

Now outside, she smiled and handed him a second beer. "Ready for another?"

His brows rose. "Sure. Thanks." As he took it, their eyes met and held, and a little zing shot through her. The usual whenever they looked straight at each other.

She turned and headed back toward the kitchen, feeling distracted and desperately trying to stay on task.

"You trying to get me drunk?"

"Maybe." She playfully tossed the word over her shoulder then ducked inside before he could respond.

Tonight was the night she hoped to get him to open up. If she had to ply him with beer to do it, she would.

Later over dinner… "Mmm, this is delicious," Carey said, tasting the cedar-infused salmon. "That lime juice brings out a completely different flavor." They sat at the small picnic table on the deck under a waxing June moon.

"Not bad, I must say. What kind of crazy food do we have to prepare tomorrow?"

"Watercress soup with anchovies, what else?" She laughed. "That's lunch, but for dinner we get chicken teriyaki with shredded veggies, oh, and cheese rolls. Can't wait for the bread!" She leveled him with her stare. "I have to thank you for putting up with this crazy diet."

His gaze didn't waver. "I've enjoyed everything so far." He reached across the table and covered her hand with his. "Since I'm your prenatal partner, the least I should do is help you stay on the diet. Your baby will thank me one day."

Sometimes he said the sweetest things and she just wanted to throw her arms around him. But she'd made that mistake once already during the self-defense training and it had mixed up everything between them for days afterwards. Since then he seemed to have shut down like a spring snare, and she'd carefully kept her distance. But he'd just planted a thought she couldn't drop. Would her baby ever know him?

Right now his hand was on top of hers, and she couldn't for the life of her understand why such a wonderful man wasn't still happily married with his own assortment of kids.

She lifted her lids and caught him still watching her, both totally aware of their hands touching, so she smiled but it felt lopsided and wiggly. She stopped immediately, not wanting him to think she was goofy looking or anything. Things felt too close, it nagged at her, and she knew how to break up that uncomfortable feeling pronto. "You mentioned once that you were divorced." She decided to get right to the heart of the conversation she'd planned to start tonight.

He removed his hand from hers and sat taller as ice seemed to set into his normally kind eyes. "Yeah." He dug into his vegetables and served himself more fish, suddenly very busy with eating. "My wife left me."

Why would any woman in her right mind leave Joe? "That must have hurt like hell."

"It was not a good time." He clipped out the words, with an emphasis that communicated it would be the end of this conversation. And why did she know without a doubt that he wasn't telling her anywhere near the whole story? Because he'd hinted at "getting it" and knowing how babies changed lives. Things didn't add up. Had he lost a child?

So she pressed on, hoping that talking about herself some more might help him to open up. "Sometimes people *should* get divorced." She pushed her empty plate away and sipped from her large glass of iced water.

"For instance, my parents were a train wreck. My dad was out of work most of the time, and my mother was always taking on whatever odd jobs she could to make up for it. Instead of being grateful, my typically belligerent father went the macho route, accusing her of thinking him not good enough to take care of the family. Occasionally he'd haul off and hit her, too. I swore I'd never, *never* put myself in the same position."

Joe protested, shaking his head. "You didn't."

"Didn't I? After working my whole life to be independent, I fell for the exact same kind of guy as my dad. A man so insecure about his masculinity that he kept me isolated, insisting it was because he loved me so much. Then he turned violent whenever I stood up to him, and especially when I told him we were going to have a baby. What a fool I was. I didn't learn a thing from my parents' lousy marriage." If she hadn't already finished eating she wouldn't have been able to take another bite, with her stomach suddenly churning and contorting with emotion.

"He must have had a lot going for him to get you interested at first, though. I'm sure he hid his insecurities really well." His hand came back to hers. "Don't call yourself stupid. You have a big heart. You just didn't see the changes coming."

"You give me a lot of credit." She squeezed his hand. "I'm still mad at myself for winding up in this position."

"As crazy as it sounds, I'm kind of glad you did." He squeezed back then let go completely, keeping things safe and distant. "You're better off here."

With you? She wanted to add, *I am better off here but where do we go from here?* "What are we, Joe?"

He screwed up his face in mock confusion. "What do you mean?"

"Are we friends? You can't call me a tenant because I'm not paying you rent." She tried to make an ironic expression, but fell far short because the next pressing question was already demanding she ask it. "Am I one huge charity case that you, in your kindness, the way your parents taught you, just can't bring yourself to send away?"

"God, no. Carey, come on." He wadded up his napkin and tossed it on the table. "You're overthinking things, making problems where there aren't any. We're friends." He shrugged.

"We can't call ourselves friends if you won't open up to me." She stood and started clearing the table. "Friends share things."

Joe shot up and helped to pick up dishes, as usual, and they headed to the kitchen and washed the plates in silence. A muscle in his jaw bunched over and over. Not only had she *not* gotten Joe to open up, she'd made sure he'd keep his distance and would probably never let her close. Major fail.

But what should she expect, being pregnant with another man's baby?

Early on Monday morning the phone rang. Sunday evening had been strained but tolerable between them, and Joe had withdrawn more from Carey by working during the day and later by working out while listening to that aggressive jazz saxophone music while he did so. It made her want to put on headphones. Carey didn't know if she could take much more of him distancing himself from her, but under the circumstances she felt trapped for now. Which felt far too familiar, considering her past.

Joe had the day off and answered, then quickly handed the phone to Carey.

"This is Mrs. Adams from social services. The police department told us about your current situation, and Helena from The Hollywood Hills Clinic Social Services also contacted us. Sorry it took so long, but there is quite a backlog. Anyway, we have found a temporary apartment in Hollywood where you can stay for now."

"Well, that's wonderful. When can I have a look?"

"You can move in this weekend, if you'd like. Or today if you need to. We have a voucher worth a month's rent and this unit has just become available. Would you like me to bring the voucher by?"

"Yes. Of course. Thanks so much."

Carey hung up having made arrangements with Mrs. Adams, glancing up to see Joe watching her skeptically. She owed him an explanation and told him exactly what Mrs. Adams had just said.

"So, if all works out, I'll be out of your hair, maybe as soon as tonight."

"Where is this place? Will you be safe?" There went that jaw muscle again.

"I don't know anything, but would social services send me somewhere unsafe?"

"They're just trying to put a roof over your head." His fingers planted on and dug into his hips, his body tensed. He wore an expression of great concern, making his normally handsome face look ominous. "Safety might not be their number-one goal. I'm going with you."

Every once in a while, thanks to her recent experience with Ross, Joe seemed too overbearing. Yeah, she'd messed up lately, but she was a big girl, a mother-to-be! And she would be in charge of her life from here on. "I can take care of myself. Thanks."

His demeanor immediately apologetic, he came closer. "I didn't mean to come off like that, dictating what I intended to do, but please let me come with you. I'd like to see where you'll be living. I know all the areas around here."

Since he sounded more reasonable, she changed her mind. "Okay, but I make the decision. Got that?"

"Got it. But first off you've got to know that you don't have to move out. You're welcome to stay here as long as you need to."

"Thank you, but as a future single mother I've got to prove to myself I can take care of things. I got myself into this situation, I should get myself out. Besides, I'll be starting the temporary job next Monday, and—"

"Your salary won't be enough to rent an apartment in any decent neighborhood. I'm not trying to throw a wet blanket on your plans, I'm just being honest."

She refused to lose hope. "I'm going to go see that apartment with Mrs. Adams and then I'll decide."

"Can you at least call her back and tell her I'll drive you over there?"

"Okay, but only because it will be more convenient for her."

"Fine."

That afternoon Joe parked on North Edgemont in front of an old redbrick apartment building that was dark, dank and seedy-looking as hell. He clamped his jaw and ground his molars rather than let Carey know what he thought. She'd made it clear it would be her decision, and he'd honor that. The only thing the area had going for it was a huge hospital a couple of blocks down on Sunset Boulevard.

If they'd offered the rent voucher the first week she'd moved in, he would have encouraged her to jump on it. Having a woman in his house again, especially a pregnant woman, brought back a hundred different and all equally awful memories. Having to do things together, like shopping for groceries and fixing meals, was nearly more than he could bear. Plus, with Carey living with him, it seemed Angela had moved back in, just in a different form. So he'd concentrated on Carey being a victim and he was her protector. Keeping it clinical and obligatory had been the key.

Best-laid plans and all, he'd gotten involved with her anyway. Why had he taken it on himself to teach her self-defense, and why in hell had he volunteered to be her prenatal class partner? The problem was there was too much to like about Carey. So he glanced at the dreary apartment building and felt a little sick.

If she decided to take this place, he'd have to find her

a car. Which wouldn't be a problem with his father's business. No way did he want her walking these streets at night, coming home from work and getting off the bus. Pressure built in his temples just thinking about it.

He stood back and let Carey introduce herself to Mrs. Adams, who showed her inside. The term *flophouse* came to mind, but Joe kept his trap shut. Damn, it was hard.

The single room had a tiny alcove with a half-refrigerator, a small microwave and a hot plate. How would she be able to continue with the nutritious meals from Gabriella's class? He'd throw out the mattress from the pullout bed and burn it rather sleep on it, and the rusty toilet in the so-called bathroom made his stomach churn. Not to mention that the constant dripping from the kitchen sink would keep her awake at night.

Caution was as plain as day on Carey's face as she glanced around the place. But he already knew her well enough to know she'd try to make the best out of a lousy situation. Hell, she'd been putting up with him withdrawing every time they'd gotten too close. Probably walked on eggshells around him. But was living with him so bad that she'd choose a dump like this just to get away?

Last night she'd said a real zinger, not realizing it, of course, but nevertheless her comment had hit hard. When she'd talked about her ex being insecure about his masculinity to the point of taking over her life, it had made Joe cringe. He could relate, especially since getting the lab results about him being sterile, and following up later with a urologist as to the reasons why. Was that part of him wanting to protect Carey? Was it some twisted way of making himself feel like a complete man again?

"And you said you have a voucher for the rent here for the next month?" Carey asked.

Mrs. Adams, a tiny African-American woman with short tight curls and wearing a bright red blouse, looked serious. "Yes, we can also provide food stamps and you can move in now or this weekend if you'd like."

Carey was about to say something, and damn it to hell if it meant he was waving around his insecure masculinity or whatever, Joe couldn't let this fiasco continue another second. "What's the crime rate in this neighborhood?" he butted in.

An eyebrow shot up on Mrs. Adams's forehead. Was she not used to being asked that question by people desperate enough to need county social services assistance? "I honestly don't know. It's a busy neighborhood. There's a church right up the street, a hospital down on Sunset. There's a small family-run market on Hollywood Boulevard and the apartment building is really well situated for all of her needs."

Carey stood still, only her eyes moved to watch him. Was it trust or fear he saw there? Was his being concerned coming off as overbearing? He hoped she saw it a different way, the way he'd intended, that he was worried for her safety. He subtly shook his head but she quickly glanced back at Mrs. Adams. "Thank you so much for showing me this place. Do I have to sign anything?"

Joe understood she'd been trying to be a good soldier, stiffening her lip and all, but all it had done was turn her to cardboard. She obviously wanted to make the offer from social services work out, but Joe strongly suspected that in her heart she was scared. And he was pretty sure he saw it in her eyes, too. Those lush meadow-green eyes seemed ready for a storm. How could she not be afraid? Now that he'd identified what was going on with her, he could practically smell that fear. He just hoped it wasn't directed toward him.

She didn't belong here. She belonged with him. Safe. Protected. That's all there was to it. Was he being crazy, like Ross? With all his heart he hoped not, but right at this moment it was hard to evaluate his motives because the lines had blurred and there was no way in hell he'd let this happen.

Joe stepped forward, unable to let the scene play out another moment. He reached for and gently held Carey's upper arm, pleading with his eyes, hoping she wouldn't see a crazed, insecure man. He fought to keep every ounce of emotion out of his voice. "Stay with me." Making the comment a simple suggestion. Then he stumbled, letting a drop of intensity slip back in. "Please."

Carey hadn't given in, though she'd wanted to. Mrs. Adams had gone on alert when Joe had taken her arm in his hand. The poor woman had probably thought he was the guy she needed to get away from. Carey had made sure she knew otherwise. No, Joe wasn't scary, but he had a rescue complex and she needed to help him get over it.

They drove back toward West Hollywood mostly in silence. True, the last thing she wanted was to move into such a depressing place, but rather than cave just because Joe wanted her to she'd asked Mrs. Adams to give her twenty-four hours to make her decision. It had also seemed to calm the woman's sudden uneasy demeanor over the battle of wills between Carey and Joe about moving.

And this had been where Joe had proved he was nothing like Ultimatum Ross. Trusting her decision, he'd agreed that was a smart idea, and Mrs. Adams had smiled again. Inside, so had Carey.

The man was too good to be true, and she couldn't trust her instinct to believe he was what he was, a great guy! She'd thought she'd fallen for a great guy back home, a man who'd gone out of his way to charm her and make her laugh, and above all who'd wanted to take care of her. Look where that had led. But the last two weeks of living with Joe had been little short of perfection. He was patient and friendly, didn't have mood swings, like Ross, had just mostly kept his distance. Sometimes that had been maddening. Joe was tidy and helpful and—oh, she'd tried long enough to avoid the next thought—sexy as hell! The male pheromones buzzing through that house had awakened something she'd tried to put on hold since long before she'd gotten pregnant. Desire.

When she'd taken off her blindfold and finally seen who Ross truly was, she hadn't wanted to be engaged to him anymore. But he was such a manipulating and suspicious guy that she'd pretended to be sexually interested just enough to keep him off the scent. She'd intended to leave him. Had made plans for it, too. Then the unthinkable had happened and she'd gotten pregnant. The only thing she could figure was she'd missed a birth-control pill. Ross had hated hearing that excuse, and he'd accused her of wanting to ruin everything they'd had together. He'd even accused her of being unfaithful.

And he'd gotten violent.

How could she ever trust her instinct where men were concerned?

She needed Joe to open up to make sure he wasn't hiding something awful. Maybe she could use him wanting to rescue her all the time as a bargaining chip to get him to share something personal. She'd been kind of forced to tell him about Ross, what with her bruises and black eye and being pregnant and running away. But her attempt to get him to tell her about his failed marriage Saturday night had fallen flat. Maybe his divorce still hurt too much.

"If you expect me to continue to live with you, we have to actually be friends, not just say we are."

"Of course we're friends." He kept his eyes on the road.

"No, we're not. I've shared some very personal stuff with you, and yet you're nothing but a mystery to me. Friends know things about each other."

"What do you want to know?" He sounded frustrated.

"Why did your wife leave you? What happened? What broke up your marriage?"

He braked a little too hard for the red light, then stared straight ahead for a couple of moments. "If you're thinking I was a player you'd be wrong. In our case it was the other way around."

Carey nearly gulped in her shock. What woman in her right mind would be unfaithful to a guy like Joe? What in the world was she supposed to say to that? "She left you for another man?" She admitted she sounded a little dumbstruck.

"As opposed to a woman?" He gave an ironic laugh and glanced at her with challenge in his eyes. "I guess that might have hurt even more, but yes to your question. It was another man." He could have been testifying in court by his businesslike manner. Just the facts, ma'am.

So Joe was one of the walking wounded, like her.

"I'm so sorry." It was probably a lot easier for him to assign himself the role of protector than to open the door to getting involved with another woman. Especially a vulnerable person like her. Joe had proved to be wise on top of all his other wonderful assets.

Though she knew without a doubt what had gone down today, looking at the apartment, was on a completely different level. Joe had asked her to stay. She'd seen from that touch of desperation in his eyes that he'd meant it, too. She didn't have a clue if once upon a time he'd asked his wife to stay and she'd left anyway, but right at this instant Carey made a decision.

No way would she be another woman walking out on Joseph Matthews. "May I borrow your cell phone?"

While driving, he fished in his pocket and handed it to her. She looked in her purse for the business card. "Hello, Mrs. Adams? This is Carey Spencer. Yes, hi. About that apartment, I am so grateful for the rent voucher and the offer of food stamps, but I have decided to stay where I am."

Not another word was spoken on the drive home, but Carey could have sworn the built-up tension in the car had instantly dissipated as if she'd rolled down the window and let the Santa Ana winds blow it all away.

The following Monday Carey started her new job as a substitute ward clerk and couldn't hide her elation over working again. More importantly, the California Board of Registered Nurses assured her she'd get her RN license in a couple more weeks, just in time to apply for another job, this one as an RN, after the vacationing ward clerk came back. Life was definitely looking up.

The evening shift on the medical/surgical unit was nonstop with admissions and discharges, and she was grateful she'd spent a couple of afternoons learning the computer software and clinic routine with the current ward clerk the week before she'd left.

Joe had offered to rent her a car, but she didn't feel ready to drive the streets of Los Angeles, especially those winding roads in the Hollywood Hills, just yet, so Joe had reworked things and scheduled himself on evening shifts so he could bring her to work and back.

She sat transfixed before the computer at the nurses' station, deciphering the admitting orders from Dr. Rothsberg for a twenty-eight-year-old starlet who'd been intermittently starving and binging herself then herbal detoxing for the last several years, until now her liver showed signs of giving out. She'd been admitted with a general diagnosis of fever, malaise and abdominal tenderness. Though bone thin everywhere else, her abdomen looked to be the same size as Carey's, but the actress wasn't pregnant.

Carey had arranged for the ultrasound and CT studies for the next day, and had moved on to requesting a low-sodium diet from the hospital dietary department, which had a master chef. She could vouch for the great food with a couple of memorable meals she'd had during her stay. The patient would probably never notice the lack of salt amidst a perfect blend of fresh herbs and spices. Then she reminded the admitting nurse that her patient was on total bed rest. She went ahead and read Dr. Rothsberg's analysis and realized therapeutic paracentesis was likely in the petite Hollywood personality's future.

Deep in her work, she glanced up to find Joe smiling at her. "I brought you something," he said, then handed her a brown bag with something inside that smelled out of this world.

She stood to take the bag over the countertop, inhaled and couldn't resist. "Mmm, what is it?"

"Your dinner. I was on a call in the vicinity of Fairfax, so I got you one of those deli sandwiches you gobbled down the last time we were there."

"Turkey salad, cranberries and walnuts with bread dressing?"

"Yup."

"Including the pickle?"

He nodded, as if offended she'd even suggest such an oversight.

"Well, thank you. I'll be starving by the time my dinner break rolls around."

"You're welcome." He got serious and leaned on his forearm, making sure to hold her gaze. "I've been thinking. We'll have to get more organized now that you're working and pack a lunch for you every day. We can still use Gabriella's guidelines."

"Sounds good." Totally touched by his concern for her well-being, she fought that frequent urge to give him a hug. Fortunately the nurses' station counter prevented it this time. "But please let me splurge on things like this once in a while." She held up the deli bag.

He winked, and it seemed a dozen butterflies had forced their way into her chest and now attempted to fly off with her heart. Since she'd decided to keep living with him, he'd changed. He'd become easier to talk to, and though he still hadn't opened up he'd quit grinding his teeth so much. Truth was, the man could only suppress his wonderful nature for so long. Now she was the lucky recipient of his thoughtfulness and loving every second of it.

"See you later," he said, making a U-turn and heading off the ward. The perfectly fitting light blue polo shirt showed off his broad shoulders, accentuating his trim waist, the multi-purpose khaki cargo pants still managing to hug his buns just right, and those sexy-as-hell black paramedic utility boots... She guiltily watched his every move until he was out of sight. Wow, it looked like she didn't have to worry about her sick relationship with Ross at the end before she'd run away, and ruining her natural sex drive. She'd faked interest and excitement with him for her safety. Now, with Joe, without even trying, the most natural thoughts of all had awakened some super-hot fantasies. Like the desire to make love and really mean it. What would that be like with Joe?

"Uh-huh. Nice." One of the other nurses in the area had joined her in staring at the masculine work of art as he'd swaggered out the door. How could a guy *not* swagger, wearing those boots?

Getting caught ogling Joe made Carey's cheeks heat up, especially after what she'd just been thinking, so she tossed a sheepish look at the nurse then delved back into the admission packet for the actress.

Joe went straight to the clinic's paramedic station just off the ER to check on the EMT staff. He knew the emergency nurses sometimes got upset if the guys didn't help out when things got busy. Joe was always prepared to intervene and explain that wasn't their job, and the RNs didn't need to get all worked up about the EMS guys sitting for half a minute, waiting for the next call. On the other hand, he'd insisted to his guys that if a nurse said she needed more muscle, and they weren't doing anything at the time, they should jump to it and help out with lifts and transfers. Keeping RNs happy was always a good idea. He'd also taken to suggesting the guys hang out in their truck on downtime rather than at the tiny desk with two computers designated as their work station, so as not to complicate things in the ER.

Not taking his own advice, he took a seat and brought up the evening's schedule, and in the process sat in the vicinity of James, who was conferring on the phone about a patient he'd just admitted to Carey's floor with liver issues. James nodded and smiled at Joe, and Joe returned the courtesy.

Soon James hung up. "How's that scar doing? Any more tearing with your workouts, you beast?"

Joe laughed. "I'm all healed. Thanks." Joe saw James's sister, Freya, appear across the ER, obviously looking for someone.

"There you are," she said over the other heads, immediately making her way toward James.

James ducked down in an obvious fashion. "Oh, boy. Here we go," he said jokingly in an aside to Joe. "What does she want this time?" He raised his voice to tease his younger sister.

Knowing from their rocky history that the brother and sister's relationship had never been better since Freya had come to The Hollywood Hills Clinic as a sought-after public relations guru, Joe chuckled at James's wisecrack.

"There you are," Freya said, her dark blue eyes sparkling under the fluorescent ER lights. "I know you've been avoiding me, but I need a firm date for when you'll visit the Bright Hope Clinic. Here's my calendar, I've highlighted the best days and times for me and them. What works for you?" She shoved her small internet tablet calendar in front of James, making it impossible for him not to pick a day and time.

Her long brown hair was pulled back into a simple

ponytail that waved down her back, nearly to her waist, yet she still looked like she could be royalty. Hollywood royalty, that was. Joe had heard rumors about her once having had to go to rehab for anorexia, but from the healthy, happy-looking pregnant woman standing before him he'd have never guessed.

James took a deep inhale and scrolled through his smartphone calendar, matching day for day, saying, "No. Nope. Not that one either. Hmm, maybe this one? September the first or the second?"

"Let's take the first." Freya quickly highlighted that day. "It is now written in stone. Do you hear me? There's no getting out of it. You'll show up and do those publicity photos in the clinic in South Central and smile like you mean it."

"Of course I'll mean it. I'm going for the children."

"I know, but you know." They passed a secret brother-sister glance, telling an entirely different story than the simple making of plans for publicity shots. Joe deduced that since Dr. Mila Brightman ran Bright Hope, she was the issue. She happened to be Freya's best friend, and also the woman James had stood up on their wedding day. Or, at least, that was the scuttlebutt Stephanie the receptionist had told Joe one day on a break over coffee in the cafeteria. It had happened before Joe had started working there, she'd said, so all he could do was take Stephanie's word for it. The woman really was a gossip. But, damn, if that was the case, no wonder James hesitated about going. How could he face her after dumping her on the day of her dream wedding?

Having achieved her purpose, Freya rushed off, no doubt wanting to end her day and get home to her husband Zack.

"The last thing I want to do is upset a pregnant lady,"

James said to Joe in passing, "but, hey, you know all about that, right?"

The casual comment took Joe by surprise. At first he thought James was referring to his ex, Angela, but then realized he must have been referring to Jane Doe, aka Carey, who lived with him and happened to be just shy of four months pregnant.

"Tell me about it," Joe said, hoping he'd recovered quickly enough not to seem like a bonehead, and pretending that pregnant ladies were indeed unpredictable and demanding, while knowing for a fact Carey was anything but.

On Friday night, at the end of the first week on the job for Carey, Joe insisted they stop for a fast-food burger on the way home. How could she have been in California for three weeks and not tried one? They didn't even bother to wait to get home but devoured them immediately on the drive. Even though it definitely wasn't on her second-trimester diet list, she'd never tasted a better cheeseburger in her life.

"My parents are having a barbecue on the Fourth of July," Joe said, his mouth half-full, one hand on the steering wheel, the other clutching a double cheeseburger.

A national holiday had been the last thing on her mind lately. Plans seemed incomprehensible. She thought of that dreary apartment she'd almost taken and shivered at the thought of being on her own there, especially on the Fourth of July, grateful to have Joe's sweet house and lovely garden in the back to look at. She'd be just fine.

"Do you want to come? They'd love to have you."

What? He was inviting her to his parents' home?

Why? Out of his usual sense of obligation? "Oh, you don't have to—"

"I want to, and my whole family's going to be there so you can meet my sisters and brothers, too."

"Do they know about me?" Why was he pushing to take her?

"I have a prying mother and a loose-lipped sister. Mom's got this sixth sense about changes in my life, no doubt recently fueled by Lori loaning out some clothes."

"The whole story?" She really didn't want her personal failures shared, especially with Joe's family.

He shook his head and took another bite of his burger. "I wouldn't do that. You know better. But you said you wanted to be friends, and I take my friends to family barbecues."

She'd put her foot down when she'd decided to stay with him. He'd agreed to consider her a friend. If this was his way of proving it, as confusing as it would be for her, not to mention nerve-racking, she really shouldn't refuse to meet his family. It might set things back if she didn't.

"Then I guess I'll have to go." She played coy, but cautious contentment she hadn't felt in ages settled in a warm place behind her breastbone. This was more proof that Joe was *nothing* like Ross. He pushed her to get out and do things, got her a job, and now he wanted her to meet his family on Independence Day no less. Wow, what did it all mean?

Joe finished his hamburger as they neared his house. It'd tasted great, as always, but now his stomach felt a little unsettled. He'd tried not to think about the ramifications of what he'd just done, but couldn't avoid it. Trust, or lack thereof, in women in general and Carey, by reason of her gender, made him have second thoughts about the invitation. The gift of Angela's infidelity just kept on giving.

Maybe he'd jumped the gun in asking her to his parents' Fourth of July party. It was too soon. She might get the wrong impression and he wasn't anywhere ready to get close to her. He pulled into the driveway and rather than pull into the garage he parked under the small carport instead. It wasn't like he could change the date of Independence Day, and for the record he wondered if he'd ever be in a place to trust a woman again, whether next week or two years from now.

But the damage had been done. He'd asked Carey to go along, and he couldn't very well take the invitation back. He'd just have to live with it.

Once home, Carey went directly to her room to change her clothes, planning to watch a little TV to unwind after another busy evening shift at the end of her first week. But not without noticing a shift in his mood since he'd issued, and she'd accepted, the invitation to his parents' Fourth of July barbecue. When she came back, Joe was already working out on the patio, hitting his punching bag like it was a full-out enemy. For someone who'd just wolfed down a double-double cheeseburger, French fries and a large soda, he looked the picture of health.

Feeling a bit guilt-ridden, she wandered into the dining room to have a better look, wondering if he'd taken his T-shirt off for her benefit. She particularly loved watching the muscles on his back ripple whenever he landed a good punch. She stood quietly, taking in the whole workout, admiring every inch of him.

Before she'd run away, she'd worried about ever having normal desire for a man again. Faking love with Ross had scarred her more than she'd ever dreamed.

But it hadn't stopped there. Ross had dominated her entire existence to the point of making her fear for her life. How could she ever desire a man who'd treated her like that?

Yet Joe, without even trying, brought out her most basic feelings. He turned her on. So confusing. Maybe she could blame that on the concussion or the pregnancy. Yet what a relief to know she was still a red-blooded woman with a normal sex drive.

With his back to her, he grunted and huffed as he punched the bag, and she could swear the muscles on his shoulders and arms grew more cut by the moment. Needing to either bite her knuckle to keep from groaning or do something to cool herself off, she chose to head to the kitchen for a bottle of water. When she opened the refrigerator, she grabbed one for Joe, too.

This time making her presence known, she went out onto the patio, setting his water near him. "You're making me feel very guilty about having that burger and not intending to do my preggers exercises tonight, you know."

Joe laughed, and because of it messed up his timing and the punch nearly missed the bag altogether. He went for the bottle. "Thanks." Carey enjoyed watching his Adam's apple move up and down his throat while he gulped the water. A few drops dribbled down his chest. Yeah, she noticed that, too.

Her eyes drifted to the jagged scar running across his ribs, still red and tender-looking. He'd been stabbed rescuing her. The thought seemed surreal and sent a barrage of intense feelings ranging from gratitude to lust to guilt rushing through her. On impulse she walked toward him, reached out and gingerly ran her fingers across the scar. His skin was damp, smooth and...

She slowly lifted her gaze from the fit washboard abs to his chest and the pumped pecs lightly dusted in dark hair, then onward to his strong chin and inviting mouth and last to his intensely brown, almost black with desire, eyes.

The moment, when they were up close and locked into each other's stare like that, shuddered through her.

Feeling absurdly out of character in general, and especially because she was four months pregnant, she ignored her insecurities, focusing only on the consuming pull between them, making a trail with her fingertips across the expanse of his muscled torso, along the broad rim of his shoulder, then upward to his jaw.

She swallowed lightly in edgy anticipation.

He didn't move, just kept willing her into the depth of his eyes, and she knew without a doubt he was as into this moment as she was. So she edged closer, lifted her chin and, though feeling breathy from nerves, she went for it, covering his mouth with a full-on kiss.

CHAPTER SIX

IF JOE LET Carey's kiss continue, he'd have to take her all the way and probably scare her half to death with his need. The mere touch of her lips had unleashed pure desire, like a lightning bolt straight down his spine.

But he knew Carey well enough now, and the woman was trying to show her gratitude for his saving her and taking her in. He didn't want gratitude, or, if she knew his whole story, pity, or anything else. All he wanted was to get lost in her body, to make love.

He broke off the kiss to get things straight. "I don't expect anything from you. You don't have to—"

She didn't listen or give him a chance to call her out, she just kissed him again, and, damn it, those lips he'd so often admired on the sly felt better kissing him than he could ever have imagined. He quit fighting his need and pulled her near, devouring her mouth, half hoping she'd get scared and back off so that what was otherwise inevitable wouldn't happen. But the hard and desperate kiss only seemed to fan her need as much as his as she pressed her body flush with his.

He could handle this, wouldn't lose control. They'd just make out for a while then call it quits. But then there was the feel of her lips, smooth, plump, that inviting-as-all-hell tongue, and the touch of her fingertips at the back of his neck and on his shoulders. The sound of her deep breathing, the scent of coconut in her hair, and especially those little turned-on sounds escaping her throat made it so hard to not completely let go. And, damn, that wasn't the only thing that was hard. Yeah, he was pumped, horny, and making out with a woman who seemed to want him as badly as he needed her.

This was about sex. Against a wall. He needed to look into her eyes, to see if she really was as into this as he was, because he wouldn't take her if she wasn't. Electricity seemed to run through his veins, maybe partly because he was worked up from boxing, but most definitely from holding and kissing her. Surely she felt that electricity too. If she was just looking for some comforting necking, she'd come on way too strong, so it was best to check things out. Figure out where she was at before he let loose. He placed his thumbs in front of her ears, his fingers digging into that thick and gorgeous auburn hair, and though hating to separate their mouths he moved her head back.

Carey seemed dazed and was breathless, so it took a moment for her to connect with his stare. Her eyelids fluttered open and maybe Joe's interpretation was skewed from wanting her so much, but her eyes were on fire. For him.

Her nostrils flared and she breathed quickly. "Please don't stop," she whispered. "This has nothing to do with gratitude, believe me." She kissed him again, and the dam of unspoken longing, secret desire, and flat-out need totally broke.

She wanted him. He wanted her. Tonight he'd have her.

He walked her backwards, reached under the back of

her thighs and lifted her as he did so. She wrapped her legs around his waist, and soon her back was against a well-secluded wall in the corner of the patio. She'd already pulled her top over her head by the time they'd gotten there, and once at the wall, just as quickly, she released her full breasts from the constraints of the bra.

He looked down. The view of their chests mashed together exhilarated him, the hot, soft feel of her breasts even better. But she was hungry for his mouth and wanted all his attention there. So he obliged. He wedged her tight against the wall, sitting her on the edge of a book case, leaning into her, weaving his fingers with hers and lifting her arms flush to the plaster so he could be closer still. She moaned, enjoying the full body contact every bit as much as he did. He inhaled her sweet-scented neck and nuzzled it deep with kisses. She liked it, moaning again and bucking her hips just above his full erection, causing more lightning bolts along his spine.

Soon Carey wiggled off his hips, standing just long enough to tug down his boxing shorts and her yoga pants. She took the time to run her hand along his glutes and give them an appreciative squeeze as she stepped up close and hugged him again.

His erection landed between their bodies and the surge of sensation from her skin to his nearly sent him over the top. God, he wanted her. And she obviously wanted him. Right then.

He may be sterile and she pregnant, but he still knew the purpose of protected sex, and it wasn't all about birth control. Any guy his age had a stash of condoms, even though lately he hadn't been in the least bit interested in getting involved enough with a woman to use them…until Carey.

Living with Carey these past few weeks had made him very much aware of where those condoms were, too. "One second." He stopped pressing her to the wall, and regretfully removed himself from between her gorgeous thighs. "Don't move." He stepped back and his eyes took her in, in all her lush splendor. God, he wanted her.

Joe zipped around the wall to his bedroom and returned in record time, afraid she might have already changed her mind.

She wasn't there. His heart sank.

"I'm in the bathroom. I'll be right there!"

The wall was looking less and less appealing so he went into his bedroom and pulled back the covers on his king-sized bed, finding it hard to believe he'd soon be making love to Carey.

Carey never had expected to be having sex with Joe tonight, but now that she'd started it, and sex was definitely on the table, or nearly against the wall in their case, she wanted to freshen up. Ross may have scarred her but Joe could heal her. She didn't expect anything more than tonight, just the chance to find out she could let go and be with him, someone new, different, better than toxic Ross. If she didn't take this opportunity, she might never get over her past or feel normal again.

She stepped into the hall to find Joe waiting for her, having made the mistake of glancing at her pregnant abdomen just before she did. A wave of insecurity nearly made her back out, but the instant she saw his Adonis-like form, and the unadulterated desire in his eyes, every insecure thought left her mind. She wanted Joe more than she'd ever wanted to be with any man.

She rushed to him and he picked her up again, her

cooler skin crashing with his hot damp flesh. She inhaled his musky scent and grew hungrier for him. He
carried her to his bed and, probably because she was
pregnant, laid her down gently. Frantic for him, she'd
have none of that, pulling him firmly toward her, and
impatiently bucked under him.

He had other plans, though, and took his time explor-
ing her body, figuring out what excited her and what
drove her wild. Just about everything at this point! On
his side, facing her, he rested on one arm, lowering
and lifting his head to kiss her mouth, her neck, her
breasts, while his free hand cupped her and explored her
most intimate area. Breathless with longing, sensations
zinging every which way through her body, she never
wanted the intensified make-out session to end. Until,
very soon, the mounting desire was too much and she
needed him, all of him, inside her.

She rolled onto her side, throwing her leg over his
hip, straddled him and pushed him back onto the mattress. From his firm feel she had zero worries whether
he was ready or not. She slid her awakened center,
thanks to his earlier attentions, along his length, thrill-
ing at the feel of it and the thought of him soon being
inside her. He'd already made her wet so she skimmed
along his smooth ridge with ease, several times, stim-
ulating herself more than she thought she could take.
He definitely liked it.

But stopping her in mid-skim, as if he might lose
control, he sheathed himself in record time then, taking control, placed her on her side with her back to
his chest. One arm was underneath her and that hand
cupped her breast while the other dipped between her
thighs and opened her, rubbing the amazingly sensitive area, and she was soon straining at the onslaught of

arousal. She moaned in bliss and Joe, being definitely ready, tilted her hips back, making her swaybacked, then entered her.

The culmination of sensations as he pressed into her took her breath away. She rolled with him, taking in every electrifying thrust. His hands remained attentive in those other strategic places as friction built deep inside, knotting behind her navel and lower. Heat lapped up the base of her spine, across her hips and over her breasts, flooding the skin on her chest and cheeks. She could feel the fully ignited body flush nearly burning her skin. If possible, he felt even harder now and an absurd thought occurred to her. She was making love with him, Joe! It wasn't a wish or a fantasy or a secret dream anymore. It was really happening.

Maybe it was the added hormones of pregnancy, and more probably it was the undivided attention from Joe, but she'd never, *ever* been this turned on in her life. With her entire body tingling and covered in goose bumps, running hot with sensations—not to mention the involuntary sounds escaping her throat—there would be no guessing on his part about how he made her feel. *Freaking amazing.*

She couldn't take more than a few minutes of the intense sensory overload without completely giving in to it. His pumping into her, slowing down and drawing out every last response, then speeding up at the perfect moment to drive her near the flashpoint soon became her undoing. She turned her head and found his mouth. They kissed wildly, wet and deep.

When she came, her center seemed to explode with nerve endings lighting up, zinging and zipping everywhere as they relayed their ecstatic message deep throughout her body. She gasped and writhed against him, riding the incredible wave for all it was worth, while sensing his time was near. Soon his low, elongated moan became the sweetest music she'd ever heard.

It had taken several minutes for things to settle down between Joe and Carey. He'd briefly jumped out of bed for the bathroom to take care of business, returning to find she'd probably done the same. He smiled when she came back with the fresh flush of lovemaking on her face and across her chest. Though she'd run a brush through her hair, it was still wildly appealing. He continued floating on the post-sex euphoric cloud when she crawled back into bed beside him. He'd just had mind-blowing sex with an amazing lady and he felt great. Beyond great. He pulled her close, delivered a sweetheart kiss then snuggled in, savoring the afterglow between them. But it was late and they'd worn each other out.

Within a few short minutes Carey fell asleep. She'd gone still, wrapped in his arms, then her breathing shifted to a slower, deeper rhythm. It felt right, holding her, breathing in her scented hair, touching her soft skin and womanly body. But sleep wasn't ready to come to Joe.

His hand dropped over her abdomen and the noticeable early second-trimester bump. It jolted him. His mind raced with comparisons with another woman and another time. He'd avoided the thought long enough, now it wouldn't let him go.

What the hell had he just done? He'd ruined everything.

The battle in his mind continued with rival thoughts. He had to be honest, he'd wanted this more than anything, and being with Carey had been on his mind for longer than he cared to admit. She'd knocked every sensible thought out of his head just by being the wonderfully appealing, sweet woman she was. The sexy-as-hell—and who'd just proved it beyond a doubt—mother-to-be.

Yes, she was pregnant with another man's baby, and though the circumstances were totally different, the scenario seemed too damn familiar.

Also, Joe worried that Carey was confusing gratitude with desire. She'd denied it when he'd bluntly asked her, but they were both obviously under some voodoo spell when it came to each other. He wouldn't dare call it love. Hell, she'd just escaped a toxic, abusive relationship. Any decent guy, and Joe considered himself one of the good guys, would be an improvement.

Back and forth he silently argued, feeding his confusion rather than solving anything. He'd essentially been acting like a partner to Carey in all but name—how had he not seen that before? It'd started with the staggering need to protect her and moved on to bringing her home. They'd lived together for almost a month, sharing the little everyday things that true couples did. He was the first person other than the midwife to see Baby Spencer in the ultrasound. He'd secretly teared up, seeing how the fetus already sucked its thumb and had a tiny turned-up nose in the profile. She'd even asked him to go to the next doctor's appointment with her, too, joking she was worried she'd forget something, and he'd been following her pregnancy like an auditor.

Just like he'd done with Angela at the beginning of her pregnancy.

What had possessed him to step into the role of being Carey's partner in the parenting class? He squeezed his eyes tight, avoiding the answer, holding her a little tighter than before. It wasn't out of pity for her being the only one enrolled without a significant other—no, he had to be honest. It was because he'd wanted to. Maybe even needed to.

Did he enjoy getting kicked in the teeth?

Damn it, for one of the good guys he was really screwed up. Losing Angela had nearly done him in, along with getting hit by the hardest dose of reality in his life. He was sterile. He'd never be a father. And Angela had cheated on him, taking the task of getting pregnant to his best friend, Rico.

In time he'd lose Carey and her baby, too, once she got back on her own two feet again. Just like he'd lost Angela and the baby he'd once thought was his for a brief but ecstatic period of time.

He slipped out of bed, unable to stay close another second to the woman who'd just thrown his entire world on its head. He pulled on his boxing trunks, went to the kitchen and drank a full glass of water, then walked to the couch and sat. Being away from her spell helped his body settle down. His mind was another story altogether, though. He folded his arms across his chest, plopped his feet on the coffee table and, using the TV controller, turned to an old black and white movie with the sound muted. Fortunately it dulled his thoughts and little by little, as the dark drama unfolded and minutes passed, he finally drifted off to sleep.

"Joe? What are you doing out here?"

Sunshine slipped through the cracks in the living-room window blinds on Saturday morning. Joe eased open one eye from where his face was mashed against the armrest cushion on the couch. "Huh? Oh, I couldn't sleep and I didn't want to wake you so I came out here."

"I was worried I'd snored or something." She'd ob-

LYNNE MARSHALL 111

viously tried to lighten the mood, so he laughed easily, as if nothing was wrong at all. She looked nearly angelic, standing with the window behind her, her silhouette outlined by bright morning light. She was wearing an oversized T-shirt with those long, slender legs completely bare. It made him want her all over again, but that was the last thing he should ever do.

"No." He scrubbed his face, trying to wake up, realizing she hadn't bought his explanation, and he needed to be straight with her. "You didn't snore." Yeah, he had to nip this in the bud and, though it might sting today, she'd thank him later for sparing her more pain.

"What's up, Joe? I don't have a good feeling about us having sex and then you sneaking off to the couch."

He wasn't ready to look at her, and when he told her his thoughts she deserved his undivided attention. "I need some coffee." He stood and she followed him into the kitchen. He glanced at her before he got on the job of filling the coffeemaker and saw the frightened and forlorn woman he'd first seen at the bus station. It made him feel sick to do that to her so he stopped avoiding the moment and grabbed one of her hands. "Look." He shook his head. "I'm sorry we crossed the line last night. It was fantastic, amazing, and a huge mistake."

"No. It was totally okay with me. Couldn't you tell?" She searched his eyes, looking for answers. It made him look down at the hand he held. "In fact, it was an incredible night. I never dreamed making love with you could be so wonderful."

He glanced upward, finding those eyes...greener in the morning light. "It was great, but things are too confused between us. You need time to heal from your lousy relationship with Ross, and the most important thing in your life right now should be your baby. Focus on the baby, instead of getting all involved with me. Not that I didn't love what we did in there last night, it's just that we're dangerous for each other right now. I shouldn't take time and energy away from you focusing on what you want to do with your life. I'll just interfere, and you need to think what's best for you, not anyone else."

Who was he kidding, laying all the excuses at Carey's feet? He still wasn't ready to trust another woman, to open up about the pain of his wife's infidelity. And that's what he'd need to do in order to be with someone new. Her. It was why he'd been living like a workaholic hermit all this time. What would she think of him if she knew how scared he was to tell her the truth, and if he wasn't ready to be completely honest, what was the point of being with her?

He pulled her close and held her, and it hurt to feel her stiffen when he wanted to love her. But now he had to push her away because she deserved better. She deserved a future of her own making. All he'd do was mess things up. "We both have a lot going on in our lives right now and it isn't a good time to confuse things even more with sex." He pulled back to engage with her eyes, but she was now the one avoiding eye contact. "And, believe me, that was incredibly hard to say, because I wanted you like I've never wanted anyone else last night."

It seemed she'd stopped breathing, a dejected expression changing her beauty to sadness. He felt queasy, like he'd already finished the pot of coffee and the acid lapped the inside of his stomach. But he forged on because he had to.

"It's not right for us to be together now. Our timing

is off. We just have to face that. And no one is sorrier than me."

Something clicked behind those beautiful eyes. Her demeanor shifted from tender and hurting to world-weary chick. "Yeah, you're right. It really was stupid." She pecked his cheek with a near air kiss. "Now I need to shower."

He watched her walk away, her head high and shoulders stiff. In that moment he hated more than anything having given her a reality check, and the thought of drinking a cup of coffee made him want to puke.

CHAPTER SEVEN

CAREY STOOD UNDER the shower, hiding her tears. Joe's rejection had stung her to the core. She'd given him everything she had last night yet this morning he had closed the door.

She lifted her head and let the water run over her face. He'd made her remember her shameful past, and she wanted to kick herself for trying to forget. If there was one lesson she should have learned by now it was not to ever let herself get close to any man again. Yet here she was a month after running away from Ross, opening her heart to Joe. Could she have been more stupid?

Joe wasn't out to hurt her. It had just turned out that way, and it was her fault. She'd suspected from the beginning that he carried heavy baggage. It may have taken a near stranglehold to get him to reveal one small fact—the tip of the iceberg—that his wife had screwed him royally, and what the rest of the story was, Carey could only guess. One thing was certain, he was hurting and afraid of getting involved again.

Truth was she wasn't the only one with a past not to be proud of. Joe belonged in her league. All the more reason the two of them were a horrible match.

Yet she'd trudged on, defying the truth, letting his

kindness and charming personality, not to mention his great looks, win her over little by little. She'd let him take care of her and he'd quickly earned her trust. She still trusted him. But she couldn't let herself fall any deeper in love with him. Something in her chest sank when she inadvertently admitted she'd fallen for him. No. That couldn't be. She needed to stomp out any feelings she already had for Joe beyond the practical, and she needed to do it now. She lived here because she couldn't afford her own place. Yet. In time she'd be free of him, wouldn't have to be reminded daily how wonderful he'd been at first. Then how tightly he'd shut her out. Yet how much she still cared for him fanned the ache in her chest.

She diligently lathered her body, aware of more tears and that sad, sad feeling nearly overtaking her will to go on. Then her hands smoothed over her growing tummy and she knew she couldn't let anything keep her from the joy of becoming a mother. Her baby deserved nothing less than her full attention. Wasn't that what Joe had said, too?

From now on she'd concentrate on getting her life together and becoming a mother, and forget about how being around him made her feel as a woman. Really, how stupid was it, anyway, that fluttering heart business. It never paid off.

After showering and hair-drying and dressing, with her mental armor fully in place, she marched into the kitchen where she heard Joe puttering around. "I've decided to take you up on that offer to rent a car for me."

"Sure, we can do that this afternoon since my dad owns a rental franchise." He responded in the same businesslike tone she'd just used on him.

"Thanks. In the meantime, may I borrow *your* car? If I don't leave now I'll be late for the Parentcraft class."

He was dressed. He stopped drying the coffee carafe, turned and looked at her dead on. "I'm going too, but you can drive if you want."

He tossed her the keys, and in her profound surprise she still managed to catch them. "Uh, I don't think so."

"Well, I know so, because you forget things. And two sets of ears are better than one, especially since you're probably already distracted from everything I pulled on you this morning."

"It would be totally awkward for both of us. You know that."

"No, I don't because I've never done this before. Besides, no one else needs to know."

He was making her crazy with this line of thinking, and so, so confused. "I can't just give myself to someone then forget about it. What's wrong with you?"

"You're right, I'm totally screwed up, I admit it, but I started this class with you, and I intend to be there for you all the way to the end."

Why was he being so unreasonable? But, honestly, how could she hold against him what he'd just acknowledged? He was the first guy in her life who insisted on sticking something out with her. It seemed a very unselfish thing to do.

Now her head was spinning, and it wasn't because of the recent concussion. "This is all too complicated. I'd rather just go myself." He'd hurt her enough for one day. She couldn't possibly sit next to him in a class for two hours and not think about what had happened. Surely he knew that. What was wrong with the man?

He touched her arm and she went still. Something told her he was about to convince her to let him go, and right this minute—*thanks a million, armor, for aban-doning me*—she felt too confused to argue.

"Carey, I know how it feels to be let down by some-one. I know you've been let down a helluva lot lately, and I respect you too much to do that with this class on top of everything else I've already fouled up."

She felt like grabbing her head and running away. "Let's just drop this. I'm going now." She turned to leave, but he stopped her again.

"Listen, I may have totally screwed up by letting my body do the thinking instead of my brain last night, but long before that... I'll be honest and say I made a prom-ise to myself about you. That first night I promised I'd look after you. And once I found out you were pregnant, I vowed to be there for the baby, too."

He took her by the shoulders, leveling his gaze on hers, delving into her eyes. She couldn't bring herself to look away. "This class is important. You need to know what Gabriella has to say. I signed on to be your partner, and I intend to stay on. We may have made a huge mistake, sleeping together so soon, but in this one thing I'm going to be the only person in your life right now who won't bail on you. Please let me go with you."

Damn her eyes, they welled up and she had to blink. The man was too blasted honorable, and she hated him for it. Hated him. "I won't be able to concentrate with you there." It came out squeaky, like she needed to swallow.

"You wouldn't be able to concentrate if I didn't go either. All the more reason for me to be there." He pat-ted her stomach. "Little baby Spencer needs us to pay attention. Now, let's go."

He gently turned her by her shoulders then nudged her in the small of her back through the door, and because she couldn't stop the stupid mixed-up tears she handed back the keys. "You'd better drive."

Carey finished the temporary job as ward clerk just in time to interview for a staff RN position in the same ward at the clinic. Having seen her work ethic already, and now that she had her RN license straightened out, they hired her on the spot. Carey was thrilled! Life was looking up. Except for that messy bit of being crazy about Joe Matthews and him being adamant about living by some code of honor. He was so damn maddening!

Ever since they'd made love, and especially after he'd explained how he'd made a promise to look after her, she'd thought she'd figured him out. Basically, he was the guy of her dreams but didn't know it yet. The next big test was to get him to realize that. The guy followed the rules, maybe hid behind them, too. She could live with that for now, but it sure was hard! No deep, dark Joe secret would scare her away. Nothing he exposed could deter her. He was a good man, and she didn't want to lose him, no matter how stubborn he was. But she had to be careful not to let on about her continued and growing feelings for him or she'd blow it. The big guy needed to be handled with the utmost care. For his own good.

Things had been very strained at the West Holly-wood house since they had "faced the facts" a little over a week ago. It seemed they'd both bent over backwards to be polite and easy to get along with since then, taking the art of being accommodating to a new extreme, but simmering just beneath the surface was the tension. Always the tension. There was nothing like confusing love with kindness and one spectacular "crossing the line" event to create that special brew. Now she'd clearly seen the error of her ways.

He thought he'd convinced her to only look out for herself and the baby, and she was! But she was also letting her heart tiptoe into the realm of love, the kind she'd never experienced before. The problem was, she couldn't let her champion paramedic know or he'd run. So the question remained, was she being the world's biggest fool or the wisest of wise women?

Only time would tell.

The nursing recruiter spent the entire first day on the new job orienting Carey and preparing her for the transition to the floor. From this day forward she'd remember July the first as her personal almost-Independence Day in California. But first she had to get through the holiday weekend, which included meeting Joe's family at their annual barbecue celebration. Why? Because he was the kind of guy who would never retract an invitation once made. Hadn't he proved that already by continuing with the prenatal classes?

Man, he irked her...in a good way.

Another reason was that purely out of curiosity she wanted to meet the family that had spawned such a unique guy as Joe. If she played her cards right, she might find out a lot more about him. As she'd predicted, so far he'd yet to renege on the invitation, but she thought she'd test the waters anyway.

"Listen," she said, on the night of July third, "I think I'll skip the barbecue tomorrow." Her heart wasn't into the excuse by a long shot. After his incredibly lame but amazingly touching reason for continuing with the parenting classes, she was curious to see how compelling he could be over Independence Day.

"But you've got to come. Mom will hound me for weeks if I back out now."

"You don't have to back out. I'm just not sure I'll go."

"If you don't go, I won't either."

"You can't play me like that."

"Play you? I just gave us both a way out. I'll tell her you don't want to come."

"So I get blamed? Oh, no. It's not that I don't want to go, it's our weird relationship I'm worried about. How would we hide that?"

"By acting like friends. We are still friends, right?"

"In some crazy bizarro-universe sort of way, yes, I guess we are. Besides, your mother would be horribly disappointed if you didn't go."

"Exactly my point."

Darn it, his logic had outsmarted hers once again. "You are so frustrating!"

"So you're saying you want to spend your first Fourth of July in California by yourself? Really?"

She couldn't argue with that line of thinking. He'd invited her into his family, an honor for sure but one that wouldn't come without questions. Probably most of the questions would come from his mother. Did she want to open herself up to that? And, more importantly, why did he? But, on the other hand, did she really want to spend the holiday by herself? "Honestly, I'd rather not be alone, but I don't want to feel on the spot either."

"Trust me, I know how to handle my family, and I promise you'll have a good time. You'll like them."

That's what she was afraid of.

"My parents live close enough to the Hollywood Bowl to see the fireworks there," he said, driving to his boyhood home. "When I was a kid I used to lie flat on my back in the yard so I wouldn't miss a thing."

Carey wasn't sure she'd be able to handle anything about today, but she smiled and pretended to be interested in his story and happy he felt like talking about it. No way would she let on to Joe how tough each and every minute spent with him was for her. She did it to hold out for a bigger reward, but so far he wasn't showing any signs of opening up or changing. Holiday Joe was still By-the-Book Joe.

Carey sat in the car, wearing red board shorts with a string-tie waist to accommodate her growing tummy, a white collared extra-long polo shirt and a blue bandana in her hair. Joe wore khaki shorts and a dark gray T-shirt with an American flag on the chest in shades of gray instead of in color. Still, the point was made. They were celebrating the Fourth of July. With his big family. Oh, joy. Cue butterflies in stomach.

Although they'd made love and had opened up to each other that one night, Carey hadn't learned one bit more about Joe's broken marriage. Evidently he was determined not to ever let her know the whole story. Because of that, she felt stuck in a holding pattern, unable to be a real friend even though he'd insisted they were, definitely not a lover but merely a person who needed a place to stay, biding her time until she could move out. Every agonizing day, since things hadn't changed, it became more evident it was time to make her break.

In the back of her mind she kept assuring herself that with her new RN salary she should be able to save up enough fairly soon to rent a small but decent apartment somewhere and then get out of Joe's hair once and for all. Yet the thought of *not* seeing him every day sent a deep ache straight through her chest. Because she still cared for him.

He glanced at her, taking his eyes off the road briefly and giving a friendly yet empty smile. If only she could read his mind. She returned the favor with a wan smile of her own. What a pitiful pair they'd become. They'd both taken to wearing full mental armor since the morning after their one perfect night. Politeness was killing them. And it hurt like hell.

Joe's parents' home turned out to be in the Hollywood Hills area, not far from Joe's house. He explained while they snaked up the narrow street that he'd grown up in a neighborhood called Hollywood Heights. She could see the Hollywood Bowl to the north and some huge and gorgeous estates to the west, wondering if he might have grown up there and was secretly rich. The thought amused her. Hey, the guy had owned his own business since he'd been in his early twenties. Hadn't he said his father owned a car rental franchise? Maybe his dad was a CEO of one of the major chains. But then they turned into a long-standing middle-class neighborhood instead, and, to be honest, Carey was relieved.

Joe had never mentioned much about his family before, beyond the sister who'd loaned some clothes. Carey thought about that as they pulled into the driveway of a beautifully kept older Spanish Revival home. The front of the one-story, red-tile-roofed house was covered in ivy with cutouts where the living-room windows were and a well-maintained hedge lined the sprawling green yard in front of two classic arches on the porch. The fact that rows of palm trees stood guard on each side of the house made her smile. So Californian.

She had no idea how long his family had lived there,

but he'd just said he'd been a kid here. That made her wonder what it would be like to always have a family home where you went for holiday celebrations.

Joe introduced Carey to his parents, who clearly adored him, and she could see that he'd gotten his soft brown eyes from his mother, Martha, and his broad shoulders and dark hair from his dad, Doug. They both grinned and immediately made Carey feel welcome, though there were questions in their gazes. She wondered if they assumed she and Joe were a couple.

The sister who'd loaned Carey clothes turned out to be named Lori, and she made a point to put it out there right off—Joe was the nice guy he was only because she'd been his middle sister by two years and had often insisted he play dress up and dolls instead of cowboys and Indians. Carey laughed and watched Joe blush, something she'd never seen before. She'd bet a fortune he'd always looked out for his kid sister and younger siblings, too.

Being an only child herself, she'd never experienced the power of a sibling, in this case to put a macho guy like Joe in his place in front of his mysterious new woman friend—who'd once been so desperate as to need to borrow Lori's clothes. Now she was dying to find out who they thought she was and, more importantly, what they thought she was to Joe.

Andrew—Drew to his family and friends—was the taller but younger brother to Joe by four years, and was a fairer version of Joe but had the narrower build of his mother. Where Joe was a muscled boxer, Drew looked more like a long-distance runner. Both looked fit but in different ways.

"We're waiting for Tammy and Todd to arrive before

we begin making ice cream," Martha said, as she gave Carey a quick tour of the house.

Carey soon found out they were the babies of the family at twenty-two, fraternal twins who still seemed to hang out with each other all the time and therefore would be arriving together. Interesting. This family believed in togetherness. Another foreign idea to Carey. Maybe that had something to do with Joe insisting they continue the parenting classes together?

The rest of the four-bedroom house gave the appearance of being lived in but with obvious recent upgrades, like a state-of-the-art kitchen and a family-friendly brick patio and neatly manicured lawn, complete with a small vegetable garden. Now she understood where Joe had probably gotten his idea for his own inviting patio and backyard. He hadn't fallen far from his family tree.

Being in this home, sensing the good people who inhabited it, caused nostalgia for something Carey would never have to sweep through her, pure bittersweet longing. She'd be all the family her baby would ever have. Their home would be each other, small but loving. She vowed her child would always feel loved, no matter where they lived. Seeing good people like Joe's parents with such love in their eyes when they looked at their adult kids gave her hope for her and the baby. She wanted it more than anything for herself, that parent-child relationship.

The moment the twins walked in with a couple of bags of groceries, everything stopped and it was clear they were the wonder kids. The light of their mother's life. Martha made over them as if they were still in their teens, and Joe raised his brows and half rolled his eyes over her ongoing indulgences. *Wow, would you look at that, the babies have just managed to go to the market all by themselves*, he seemed to communicate with that look. Since she and Joe had a strong history of nonverbal communication, she was willing to bet on it. Come to think of it, Lori and Drew had exactly the same expression, and it made Carey smile inwardly. Nothing like a little friendly sibling rivalry, something she couldn't relate to. She also found it interesting that Tammy had dark hair like her father and Todd was nearly a blond—the only one in the family.

"Let's get that ice cream going," Doug said, clapping his hands, reminding Carey of Joe. He grabbed Todd, since his shopping bag contained the essential ingredients, putting him immediately on ice-cream duty. Joe was assigned to grill the burgers on the gorgeous built-in gas stainless-steel barbecue on the patio, and Lori enlisted Carey to help put together some guacamole dip and chips to go along with cold sodas and beers for those partaking, as an appetizer. Except, coming from Illinois, Carey didn't have a clue how to make guacamole, so all she actually wound up doing was mashing the avocados and letting Lori take over from there. With Martha overseeing the condiments and side dishes, already made and waiting in the refrigerator, the early dinner preparation seemed to run like a well-oiled machine.

Carey felt swept up, like a part of the family, and she cautioned herself about enjoying it too much. These were Joe's people, she'd never be a part of them. Today was simply a gathering she'd been invited to take part in rather than be left alone on a huge national holiday. If there was one thing to be sure of in these otherwise confusing days, Joe was way too nice a guy to let that happen. Yet, curiously, no one else had brought a date.

His mother loved to tell tales about her kids, embar-

rassing or not, she didn't care. It was clearly her priv-
ilege to share as their mother. Carey learned a whole
history of childhood mess-ups and adventures for all
five of the Matthews kids as the afternoon went on.
Then Lori took her aside and asked her a dozen questions about what it was like to be unconscious for three
days. They wound up having a long conversation, just
the two of them, and Carey could see herself making
friends with Lori if given the chance. It made her feel
special to be taken in so easily, and closer to everyone—
a sad thing since she understood there would never be a
chance to really be close to any of them beyond today.
Unless Joe came to his senses.

Later, as they ate, Carey found out that Drew's lady
friend was in the navy and was currently deployed in
Hawaii. Poor thing, he'd said with a grin, and just as
quickly notified his parents he was planning to take a
trip to see her in August if his dad would be willing to
give him the time off. Hmm. Carey wondered if anyone else worked for their dad.

Just as Carey prepared to take a bite of her thick and
delicious-looking home-grilled cheeseburger, which required both hands to hold the overfilled bun, a gust of
wind blew a clump of hair across her face. Before she
could put down the burger to fix it, Joe swept in and
pulled the hair out of her face, tucking it behind her
ear, a kind but cautious glint in his eyes. The simple
gesture was enough to give her shivers and make her
once again long for that dream she'd had to tuck away.
Fact was, the guy couldn't resist coming to her rescue.
Plus at his parents' house they couldn't very well hide
out in their separate bedrooms, avoiding each other.

Why did things have to be the way they were? Why
couldn't they just go for it? She took the bite of seri-

ously delicious burger, Joe having cooked them to perfection, her mind filled with more secret wishes. But even as she wished it she knew that between the two of them, with all the baggage they held on to, the fantasy of being Joe's woman would probably never be.

Lori, a yoga instructor, soon explained that her significant other was a resident at County Hospital and couldn't get the day off. Martha mentioned that Todd and Tammy would be seniors at the University of Arizona and were living at home for the summer. It made Carey feel like a special person to have the entire family to herself. And they all truly seemed to enjoy having her there.

"This is the most delicious peach ice cream I've ever tasted," she said later to Todd when the homemade dessert was served.

"It's my dad's secret recipe. He wants to make sure I carry on the family tradition."

It made Carey wonder if only the men got to learn the peach ice-cream recipe and she glanced at Joe, her unspoken question being, *Do you know how to make it, too?*

Incredibly, he gave a nod. She looked at Lori, who shook her head. Then she glanced at Drew, who'd made eye contact with her and nodded. Cripes, this intuitive communication business must run in the family, and evidently only the guys got the ice-cream recipe.

"Before you call me sexist." Doug spoke up, obviously noticing all of the subtle communication going on. The mental telepathy gift was beginning to creep Carey out! "I have my reasons," Doug continued. "It's to make sure that once a lady tastes this ice cream, she'll love it so much she'll never be able to leave one of my boys." He gave a huge, self-satisfied grin over the explanation that Carey couldn't argue with. Obviously it had worked with Martha. And from the taste of it, she understood perfectly well why. It was also very apparent Joe had never thought to make any for her.

Then it hit her that Joe's wife had left him, peach ice cream or not, and putting her own feelings aside she worried that Doug had inadvertently brought up a touchy subject for Joe. She glanced at him as he studied his bowl of dessert, though he'd stopped eating it. Martha seemed uncomfortable, too, and sent those unhappy feelings Doug's way through a terse look.

The family was well aware of Joe's heartache, and that was probably why they'd been so delighted he'd brought her over today. Oh, if they only knew how disappointed they'd soon be, but that would be nothing near what she already felt. If only...

As the afternoon wore on into evening one by one the siblings made excuses to leave, and soon it was only Joe and Carey hanging out with Doug and Martha.

"Over the years the trees in the neighborhood have grown so high they block out a lot of the view of the Bowl fireworks." Martha seemed compelled to give Carey a reason.

"I thought you said you could watch the fireworks from your backyard?" she said when she had Joe alone at one point.

"The really big ones we still can, but everyone has plans, you know how that goes."

She guessed she understood, but the thought of families, like trees, outgrowing themselves made her feel a little sad. It didn't seem to faze Martha and Doug, though. After all, the twins would be home for the entire summer.

It amazed Carey that after spending only one afternoon with the Matthews clan she already felt she knew more about their open-book world than she did about Joe, having lived with him for over a month.

"We're staying, though, right?" To be honest, Carey looked forward to seeing those famous Hollywood Bowl fireworks from his family's backyard.

"We sure are." His beeper went off and he checked it. "Excuse me." He got up, walked toward some bushes and made a return call.

She figured it was work related and suspected she might not get to see any fireworks at all today. Her sudden disappointment quickly dissipated when Joe smiled at her.

"Guess what? I've just received a special invitation."

"To what?"

Joe winked. "I must be doing really well at the clinic because James himself just invited me and a guest to his private fireworks viewing tonight."

"At his house?" A flash of pride for Joe made the hair on Carey's neck stand on end, further proving she was still far too invested in the guy. "Why so last minute?"

A satisfied smile stretched Joe's lips, the ones Carey had secretly missed kissing. By the way she'd longingly glanced at them just now, she'd probably just given herself away. "Well, apparently someone cancelled, and I was the first person he thought of."

"So you're a replacement?"

"I'd rather not put it like that but, yeah, I guess I am."

She wanted to hug him. "I didn't mean to burst your bubble. It's really a big honor."

"I know. I've heard that every year he invites a handful of employees to share the evening with him. It's sort of his way of giving a pat on the back to his best-performing department heads." Pride made his smile bright, and Carey quickly realized how rarely he grinned. If only she could put a smile like that on his face again. She had, that one special night.

"That's fantastic, Joe." Without thinking, she touched his arm, immediately being reminded of and missing the feel of his strength. "You're a hard worker and it's good that Dr. Rothsberg has noticed."

He covered his pride with a humble shrug. She wanted to throw her arms around him, but he'd made it very clear that he was never going to let her near again. Yet she'd had a wonderful afternoon and evening with his family and really liked every single one of them, feeling closer to him because of them, and a secret dream to be a part of his life rose up, refusing to get brushed aside again. Stupid, stupid girl.

Joe knew better than to push things any further than they already had, after spending the entire afternoon with Carey and his family. But he'd had a great day. Carey had fit right in with everyone, and they all clearly liked her. It made him wonder if he'd made the right decision to never let anything further happen between them. In so many ways she was right for him. It was all the stuff from before that kept both of them hung up. He hated to admit how scared he was, because it seemed so damn wussy, but he was. And Carey had wounds and scars of her own, yet she seemed more willing to move beyond them than he was. Being here with her made him feel confused again. Needing to keep his distance but not wanting to completely let go.

And here she was, in his old backyard, smiling at him. The Tiki torches lining the patio emphasized the red in her beautiful auburn hair and made her eyes look as green as the lawn. He couldn't seem to stop himself from making another big mistake where Carey was concerned. Knowing he really shouldn't open the door for more, James had told him to bring Carey along when he'd mentioned where he was and who he was spending the holiday with. And right now he couldn't think of a single reason not to.

Letting the moment take control, Joe made a snap decision. "Will you come with me?"

At a quarter to nine Joe pulled into the designated employee parking lot at The Hollywood Hills Clinic, the huge, lighted building as alive with activity as ever. Hospitals never got to take days off, but Carey was grateful she had this one Monday before she started her new job.

He directed Carey to a mostly hidden employees-only elevator by putting his hand at the small of her back. His touch made her tense with longing. *Stop it! Don't get your hopes up.*

Soon they were on the top floor, walking down a long, marble-tiled hallway. Joe opened huge French doors at the end and they stepped onto a balcony. She immediately heard music and loud talking coming from above. In the corner of the small balcony was a spiral staircase leading to the roof. Joe took her hand to show the way. Again, touching him like this set off a million unwanted feelings and emotions with which she wasn't ready to deal. Fortunately, the spectacle of a group of highly gorgeous people on the roof quickly took her mind off that.

Wow! The panoramic view of the entire city of Los Angeles was spectacular from up there, too.

Dr. Rothsberg, the tall and handsome, blue-eyed blond, golden boy of medicine, immediately came to greet Joe. "Hey, great, you could make it." He turned to Carey. "I'm so glad you could come, too."

"Thanks for having me." Carey tried to hide her fascination with the incredible specimen of a man but was worried her dazed stare may have given her away.

Dr. Rothsberg kept smiling as though he was used to people looking at him like that. "Make yourselves at home. There are drinks over there." He glanced at Carey. "No alcohol for you, young lady."

She laughed, perhaps a little too easily, wondering if all women acted this way around the guy, then figuring, *Hell, yeah.*

Joe led her to the bar and got her a root beer, already knowing her weakness for that particular soda, while he grabbed an icy IPA because it wasn't everyday he got a chance to enjoy an imported Indian pale ale.

"See that lady over there?" Joe pointed out a beautiful woman with hair a similar color to Carey's. She nodded. "Her name is Dr. Mila Brightman and she runs a clinic in South Central L.A. It's called Bright Hope. She used to be engaged to James." He'd lowered his voice and moved closer to her ear so she'd better hear him say the last part.

Carey's eyes went wide. It was hard enough being around Joe after only spending one incredibly beautiful night with him, so what must it be like to be on the same rooftop as an ex-fiancé? "What happened?"

"I don't like to spread gossip, but I heard from Stephanie the receptionist that he stood her up at the altar."

Holy moly! Why would she come close to the man if that was true?

"She's best friends with Freya, James's sister," Joe continued.

"Oh, I met Freya one day in the recruiter's office. She's our PR lady, right?"

Joe nodded.

"That should make for some heavy family tension. Wow."

"You've got that right."

He'd moved closer to bring Carey up to date without sharing the info with anyone else, and she'd moved in because of the music and talking, and now they huddled together, sipping their drinks and taking in the incredibly romantic skyline of L.A., and it suddenly overwhelmed her. They'd gotten too close. She couldn't handle it.

"I'm going to get one of those delicious-looking cookies I saw over there." She pointed to a dessert table in a secluded corner that promised to be both a delight and a nightmare for a woman monitoring her baby weight. "Can I bring you one?"

Joe shook his head, a look she couldn't quite make out covering his face. Was he sorry she'd stepped away? Or was he shutting down again? After such a great day, she hoped not.

She crossed to the spread of goodies and wound up having a harder time than she'd thought, making a decision. There was so much to choose from!

On the walk over she'd noticed Dr. Rothsberg surreptitiously watching Mila, who was across the roof, talking to Freya. Then Mila wandered over to the dessert table and stood next to Carey, and though she gave a friendly enough greeting, the woman seemed totally preoccupied with the group where James stood. As Carey continued to decide which two goodies to choose—she'd increased her limit upon seeing all the choices—Dr. Rothsberg also headed for the table.

Not having anything to do with the couple but now knowing their history thanks to Joe via Stephanie,

Carey got nervous for both of them as well as for herself. Yikes. What would happen when they faced each other? She kept her eyes down, studying the huge display of desserts, unable to make a choice or move her feet, willing herself to become invisible.

"Mila," James said, all business, "I'm sure Freya has told you I'll be coming to your clinic for a personal tour in early September."

Carey had wound up being between the two of them but on the other side of the table, and didn't dare move. They didn't seem to notice her anyway, as their eyes had locked onto each other. She chanced a glance upward to see for herself. *Yowza*, she could feel the tension arcing between them, so she distracted herself by first choosing a huge lemon frosted sugar cookie.

"Yes, Freya mentioned it. So thoughtful of you to tear yourself away from your girlfriend to make the trip."

Could the woman have sounded *more* sarcastic? But who could blame her? She'd been stood up on her wedding day. He was lucky she didn't pull a dagger on him! Carey worked to keep her eyes from bugging out and began to slice a large piece of strawberry pie in half so as not to feel too guilty about gobbling it all down. It had whipped cream topping with fresh blueberries sprinkled over it, so it was definitely a patriotic pie. Really, she *should* eat it. For the holiday's sake.

James moved dangerously close to Mila, a woman who looked like she'd claw out his eyes if he got even an inch nearer, and yet he leaned down with total confidence, his mouth right next to her ear. "In case you're interested, I've broken up with her."

Carey couldn't help looking up, but only moved her eyes so they wouldn't see body movement, still praying she was invisible, but the couple didn't seem to see her or care that she could hear their entire conversation. Mila was clearly flustered by his comment. She obviously hadn't known he'd broken up with the other woman. Wow...oh, wow.

Practically impaling Mila with his piercing blue eyes, now that he'd noticed her surprised reaction, he went still. "In the future, why don't you ask me personally how things are going in my life, instead of relying on the gossip pages as your source of information?" The sarcasm was sprinkled over every single word, yet Carey got the distinct impression that a pinch of hurt had been mixed in. She wanted to gasp over their hostile encounter but kept her mouth shut rather than draw attention to herself.

Then she accidentally dropped the knife. They both noticed. "Sorry," she said as she grabbed the pie, put it on the plate with the cookie and rushed away, wondering why Freya hadn't told Mila that James had broken up with his girlfriend, since they were best friends.

She arrived back where Joe stood, casually talking to another employee she'd seen around the clinic over the last couple of weeks. Frank, was it? They said hello and the man seemed friendly enough. Her hands shook as she took the first bite of the cookie. She glanced over her shoulder back to the dessert table but Mila and James had moved away to their respective groups. Even while trying to hide, she'd felt their sexual chemistry.

James may have stood Mila up, an unforgivable thing to do, but Carey could've sworn she'd glimpsed lingering love in his eyes. And though Mila had come off like a hurt and still angry woman toward him, Carey was pretty sure she'd seen relief on her face when James had told her he'd broken up with whoever that other woman was. Then again, Carey did have a huge imagination where love was concerned and may have seen what she'd wanted to see. She glanced at Joe, still chatting with Frank, remnants of her own lost before it ever started love driving home the point.

She promised to keep everything she'd just heard to herself. No way would she want that gossip Stephanie to get hold of this juicy information.

At exactly nine, as if some great force had waved a magic wand, fireworks started popping up all over the valley from the Hollywood Bowl, all the way out to Santa Monica beach. Someone shut off the outdoor lights as the magical display continued. Amazing and mesmerized, having never seen anything as spectacular in her life, Carey stood closer to Joe, and his arm soon circled her waist, and her arm wrapped around his. So natural. And right now there was no fighting her attraction to the man. The constant effort from living with him, plus spending all day long with him today, and especially now with a night filled with sparkles and shimmering colors dripping down the sky, had worn her down. She secretly savored his sturdy, steady build.

Carey gazed up at Joe, who beamed like a kid, nothing like that dutiful mock smile he'd given on the drive to his parents' house earlier today. She offered a bite of the fabulous cookie and was surprised when he took it greedily. Knowing this moment would only complicate things further between them, she ignored caution and leaned into his strength. His fingers gripped her side the tiniest bit tighter and her own version of pyrotechnics exploded in her chest. Yes, this would definitely confuse things. Their eyes locked for an instant. Along with seeing the reflection of fireworks in his darkened gaze, she was pretty sure she saw some regret.

Oh, who was she kidding? She'd just read her own

feelings into those wonderful brown eyes, just like she'd done with Mila and James. She really needed to stop projecting her thoughts and feelings onto everyone else. It would never get her anywhere, just make her feel disappointed. Because no matter how much she might want a second chance with Joe, it didn't matter. He wasn't open to it. But why did he keep glancing at her during the fireworks show? And now his fingertips lightly stroked her side. Funny how holidays could do that to people.

She went back to watching the dazzling and dizzying display of colors across the night sky and became aware of a strange sensation inside her. Had she eaten too much sugar? Or were the gunshot-like sounds of the rainbow-colored rockets popping and crackling through the night causing the reaction?

The feeling was very subtle, yet she couldn't deny it. This had to be *quickening.* She'd learned in her class with Gabriella that primigravida mothers often didn't realize it the first time their babies moved. Who knew? Maybe it had happened before and she'd missed it. But not this time! *Oh. My. God.* Her baby was alive and moving. *Inside. Her.*

"Joe." She nearly had to yell for him to hear her.

Grinning from the bright chaos playing out before them, he glanced down at her. When she knew she had his full attention, she was so excited she could hardly get out the words. "I just felt the baby move for the first time." Her throat tightened with emotion as she admitted it, and the unrelenting firework display went blurry in the background.

His eyes widened and his childlike grin from the fireworks turned to an amazed smile, as if she'd just told him "their" baby had moved. There she went, projecting again. But, in her defense, they had just gone over the information at the last prenatal class. Joe had been there with her, like he'd promised.

He grabbed her full on, pulling her close, then squeezed. "That must feel amazing."

Thankful for his goodness, and her good fortune of feeling her baby move for the first time on the Fourth of July, the blurriness turned to tears. "It did. Oh, my God. How strange and wonderful." She sucked in a breath, feeling like she was floating on air, then pulled away from his shoulder.

His eyes had gone glassy and the dazzling lights sparkled off them as he turned serious. She could have sworn she'd seen a flash of pain, but he quickly covered it up. He shook his head as if amazed and unafraid to show it. Just like the day in the clinic when she'd come to and nearly the first thing she'd asked had been if her baby was all right, and the nurse had assured her it was. She'd cried with joy. So had Joe. The stranger who'd saved her.

He was anything but a stranger tonight. He was the greatest guy she'd ever met.

She hugged him again and promised herself she'd remember the priceless expression on Joe's face for the rest of her life. Then she cried once more as a pang of longing for what she could never have set in deep and wide.

CHAPTER EIGHT

THEY DROVE HOME from the party in silence, still riding the high from the fireworks. Joe kept his confusion to himself. He'd held her in his arms again, and the longing had dug so deep he'd been unable to completely hide it. He was pretty sure she'd noticed his reaction, too. He couldn't continue with Carey like this. She didn't belong to him, her baby wasn't his. She deserved some guy who could love her and give her more children. Not him.

Yet she'd fit in so well with his family, and it had been clear they'd all liked her. It'd made him wonder about possibilities, and he thought he'd given up on those ages ago. Could he actually get over being cheated on by his wife and best friend, or the fact he was sterile? Was he ready, maybe, to finally move on? In his usual rut, the answer came glaring back. No.

Holding her, watching the fireworks together had been a huge mistake. Hell, ever letting her into his life had been a mistake. He'd been the one to point out how much they both had going on personally, and how important it was not to confuse things between them any further. Yet he hadn't had the heart to un-invite her for the Fourth of July celebration with his family. He'd resorted to using the lame excuse of protocol as the reason. Yeah, he was a guy of his word. Besides, his mother wouldn't have let him, and if he hadn't brought Carey, Mom would have spent the entire afternoon badgering him.

Carey's baby had moved, and the truth had knocked him sideways. She had a life to look forward to and she didn't deserve having a guy like him hold her back. Maybe one day he'd be able to forget and move on, but he wasn't there yet, and most days he doubted he ever would be. Their timing sucked. She pregnant. He like one of those zombies on the show they liked to watch together.

If he insisted on continuing to look after her, his job from now on would be making sure she became independent of him. Not to get swept away and continue to confuse and complicate things by grabbing her under the fireworks and holding her like she belonged to him. What the hell had he been thinking? From now on he had to act logically and realistically. It was his only defense for survival. And he really needed to stay out of her way.

Getting her the car from his father's lot had been a start. She could have it as long as she needed it. Now that he knew she'd be working from seven a.m. to three p.m. at the clinic, he'd go in tomorrow and change his schedule to work the evening shift.

The less time he spent near Carey, the better. The alternative was too damn painful.

"Thanks for everything," Carey said once they'd gotten home. She lingered in the living room, a dreamy smile clinging to her face.

He'd been so wrapped up in his thoughts he'd almost forgotten she was there. "Oh. Sure. You're welcome. It was fun." He shoved his hands in his back pockets and kept his distance.

"The best fireworks I've ever seen."

His attempted smile came nowhere near his eyes. "Me too." Empty words. He may as well be talking to a stranger, and she obviously felt his detachment because her expression turned businesslike.

"Well, I'd better get right to bed since tomorrow is my first day on the new job."

He tried a little harder to be part of the human race. "I'm glad you had a good time."

Her eyes brightened. "I loved your family."

That's what he'd been afraid of. "I could tell they really liked you, too." It didn't matter, he needed to step back and let her move on. Without him. "Oh, and good luck tomorrow."

She flashed that genuine killer smile and it took him by surprise. Why did it always do that? Taking every single crumb he offered, she struck him as beautiful and innocent. The sharp pang of longing nearly made him grimace. All he wanted to do was grab her and kiss her, and let his body do the thinking for the rest of the night, so he stayed far across the room, hands shoved in his pockets, and worked on making his smile look halfway real. She noticed his awkwardness and pulled back.

"So good night, then." She turned and headed for her room, her beautiful auburn hair forcing him to watch every step of her departure. That constant ache inside his chest doubled with the inevitable thought.

"'Night," he muttered. *Get used to it, buddy, soon enough she'll be walking right out of your life.*

At the end of the first week of Carey's new job, Joe, after agonizing over how best to handle the situation, told her he had to work on Saturday and would have to miss the next Parentcraft class. His intention was to let her down easily, yet he still dreaded it.

In truth, he'd scheduled the extra shift after he'd talked to Gabriella about helping Carey find a birth coach. He couldn't be the one. The thought of going through labor with her, being there for her at the toughest time, seemed beyond him. He worried he might have an emotional setback because of it, and fall apart on her. Angela and Rico had really done a job on him. He also understood how important it was for a mother-to-be to bond with their birth coach when it wasn't the husband or partner. They'd gone over that very topic the Saturday before. The sooner she found one, the better.

When he got home late that afternoon he saw Carey out on the patio deck, napping on one of the lounging chairs. Though he knew he shouldn't, he tiptoed to the screen door and studied her up close, afraid to breathe so as not to wake her. A real sleeping beauty. It brought back memories of sitting by her hospital bed, watching her, when she'd been unconscious for those three days.

Joe remembered trying to imagine who she was and where she belonged then. Now he knew exactly who she was, how wonderful she was, and how much he wanted her for himself. What a stupid fantasy. He may as well try to sprint to the moon.

She must have felt his presence or she'd been playing possum all along because he turned to leave, then heard her stir.

"Joe?"

"Yeah." He stopped in mid-step. "Didn't want to disturb your nap."

She stretched and yawned, and he didn't dare go out there, just stayed bolted to the floor, wishing things could be different. Knowing they never could be. Yearning to make it so anyway.

"What time is it?"

"Almost five. Want me to get dinner started?"

She swung her legs around and sat, feet on the wooden planks, facing him. "I missed you in class today. We started practicing relaxation techniques and special exercises. She had us work with our partners, but Gabriella worked with me."

"I had to accompany a transfer patient on the helicopter to Laguna Beach today." He'd volunteered. Would he have been able to function getting up close and personal with her in class? He'd definitely made the right decision to work, but he wondered when he'd started becoming a coward.

"The thing is, I talked to Gabriella about our situation, and she said she has access to the local doula registry. Those women love to be birthing coaches, so I asked her to give me some names." She stood and walked toward the screened-in porch door, each standing on opposite sides of the thin barrier. "Bottom line, you don't have to come anymore." With sadly serious eyes, she watched and waited.

He'd wanted to let her down easily because he was a coward. Now she'd beaten him to the task, officially releasing him. He didn't have the right to feel hurt, hell, he'd wanted a way out, but the casual comment—*you don't have to come anymore*—cut to the bone. An ice pick could have done the job just as well.

He resisted reacting, but his skin heated up anyway. He wondered how much she'd told Gabriella about them, if her story fit in any way, shape or form with his. He hadn't expected to feel upset, but he was really bothered, and definitely sad now that she'd come out and said it. Ah, hell, truth was it killed him to stand aside, even though he'd already set the ball in motion to arrange this very thing. He hadn't expected to feel like the air had been kicked out of his lungs and feel a sudden need to sit down. He steadied himself, because he knew one fact that couldn't be denied. "I guess that's for the best."

Clearly feeling let down, if he read her sudden drooping shoulders right, she covered well, too. Just as he had. "Yeah. I guess so, but thanks for being there for me all these weeks."

They'd been reduced to communicating in robotic trivialities.

"You're welcome. It was fun." *While it lasted, which he'd known from the beginning couldn't be long.* He'd just never fathomed the profound pain that would be involved. He'd gotten swept up in emotion and carried away that first Saturday, letting his feelings for Carey blur reality. He couldn't let her be the only one without a partner. He'd let down his usual guard, acted on a whim, and had paid for his mistake every single week since. Sitting beside her, acting like they were a couple, wishing it was so, scaring himself with the depth of desire for it to be so, but knowing, always knowing, it could never be.

His mouth went dry with unexpected disappointment. He needed to get away from her now. "Hey, listen, I'm going to the gym. Don't hold up dinner for me, okay? I'll grab something on the way home."

He left without before he could see her reaction.

The next Friday, Carey admitted a late-afternoon patient. The forty-eight-year-old male had a face everyone who'd ever gone to a movie or watched a TV show might recognize, but no one would know his name. The character actor had been admitted with the diagnosis of severe acute pancreatitis. Basically the guy's pancreas was digesting itself thanks to an overabundance of enzymes, in particular trypsin. His history of alcohol abuse—according to Dr. Williams, the doctor who'd been the attending doctor for Carey, and who she had enormous respect for—had made a major contribution to his current condition. However, according to the doctor's admitting notes, they would do studies to rule out bacterial or viral infection as a possible source as well.

Carey found the computer notes fascinating, and Dr. Williams had left no stone unturned. She'd even commented on the fact the man was almost fifty and still extremely buff. Probably because of his need to stay fit for the action/adventure roles he normally took, Carey decided. But getting back to the doctor's notes, she intended to consider his possible use of steroids as well.

To add another angle, when Carey did the admitting interview, the actor, who also did his own stunts for most movies, told her he'd had an accident on the job and had sustained blunt abdominal trauma. Well, that wasn't how he'd put it—*I got kicked in the gut*—but Carey's notation was worded that way. She put a call in to Dr. Williams to inform her.

Carey often thought how the practice of medicine was like a huge mystery where patients arrived with symptoms and the doctor's job was to gather all the evidence and figure out what was going on. Carey knew the clinic staff's job with this patient would be to watch for fluid and electrolyte imbalance, hypotension, decrease in blood oxygen, and even shock. This guy with the affable smile but pained brow was not to be taken lightly. Like many in the clinic, he was fit and healthy looking on the outside but a mess on the inside. These days, Carey could relate perfectly to that, too.

He'd been complaining of severe abdominal pain for a day or two, and had assumed it was because he'd been kicked in the gut, as he'd described it. Carey noted his abdominal guarding when she made a quick but thorough admitting physical assessment, and found his abdomen to be harder than usual. Of course, that could be due to the fact the man looked like he did hundreds of crunches a day. He'd said his symptoms had gotten worse in the last twenty-four hours, and had told her he felt "sick all over" so he'd come to the clinic's ER. After a few more questions he'd also admitted to going on a drinking binge a few days back. Yet somehow the guy was tanned and youthful looking for his age, until she looked closer. The saying about the eyes seemed true, and they were the mirror to, if not his soul, his health. There she could see the lasting effects of his living extra-large for many years.

His admitting labs showed his amylase and lipase levels were over the top, and that alone could have gotten the guy admitted. Add in the bigger picture, and this actor's next gig turned out to be the role of a hospital patient.

Carey inserted an IV to be used for medications as well as parenteral nutrition since he was on a strict NPO diet. Next she needed to perform a task no patient ever wanted to go through, at least from her experience as an RN. She had to insert a nasogastric tube.

"This is more to help relieve your nausea and vomiting than anything else," she said calmly. "You'll thank me for it later."

He gave her a highly suspicious stare, especially when she gave him a cup of ice chips.

"Suck on these when I tell you," she said as she manipulated the thick nasogastric tube with gloved hands and approximated externally how deep it would need to go to reach his stomach. "Okay, now."

He took a few ice chips and sucked at the exact time she used his nostril to insert the well-lubricated tube and push past the back of his throat and down into his esophagus and all the way to his stomach. His sucking on the ice would prevent her from going into his lungs. He gagged and protested all the way but didn't fight her. He gave no indication of the tubing mistakenly going into his lungs by having shortness of breath or becoming agitated, but she did the routine assessment of the placement anyway. She listened through her stethoscope as she inserted a small amount of air with a big syringe into a side port of the NG tube, hearing the obvious pop of air in his stomach when she did so.

"You did great," she said as she taped the tubing in place on his cheek and attached the external portion to his hospital gown, then connected the end to the bed-side suction machine. He gave her the stink eye, but she knew he was playing with her so she crossed her eyes at him. "It's one of the perks of my job. You know most nurses have a tiny sadistic side, right?"

That got a laugh out of him, and she figured she'd tortured the guy enough for now, even though she knew he was lined up for all kinds of extra lab work and additional tests in the next twenty-four hours. So she made sure the side rails on his bed were up and the call light was within his reach, then prepared to leave. "Get some rest."

"Like I can!" he managed to say.

"Carey?" Anne, the ward clerk she'd covered for while she'd gone on vacation called her name just as she exited the patient room.

"Coming." Carey marched to the nurses' station to see what her co-worker needed, only to find a huge vase of gorgeous flowers sitting on the counter. Lavender asters, golden daisies, orange dahlias, and roses, oh, so many perfect roses! "Wow, where'd these come from?"

"They're for you!"

"What?" Joe? What was he trying to do, make up for bailing on the parenting class? Why go back and forth like this, mixing her up even more? Ever since he'd said all those things about not confusing their living situation by getting involved with each other, and especially after the Fourth of July when he'd introduced her to his family, and especially later when they'd shared that significant moment during the fireworks, he'd been avoiding her like crazy. It'd stung and confused her, and she was only just getting her bearings back, thanks mostly to having the new job and not seeing him nearly as often. Was he feeling guilty for leading her on or letting her down? Both? She wanted to pull her hair out over his inconsistency.

Carey searched for a card, but all she found was an unsigned note.

These flowers are as lovely as you.

Sorry, Joe, but that is just inappropriate. Either you want to be involved with me or you don't. You can't have it both ways!

Hadn't he learned in the parenting class that hormones during pregnancy made every emotion ten times stronger? This tug-of-war with her feelings had to stop.

"Do you mind if I take a short break?" she asked one of the other nurses who'd begun to gather around the spectacle of colorful blooms, admiring them. The more she thought about those flowers, the more upset she got.

"Sure. I'll cover for you."

"Thanks." Carey marched to the elevator and pressed the "down" button, got off on the first floor and headed toward the ER. It was after two, and she knew Joe had been avoiding her by working the afternoon shift from two to ten p.m. in case he actually thought he was fooling her. Her eyes darted around the room until she spied him over by the computers, so she trudged on, determined to get some things straight.

"You got a second?" she asked.

"Sure. What's up?" His hair was a mess. Had he not even combed it? Her first thought was how endearing it made him look, but she stomped it out the instant she thought it. There was no point.

She had to admit the guy didn't have the self-satisfied look of a man who knew he'd just surprised a lady with flowers. "Did you send those flowers?"

He pulled in his chin, brows down, nose wrinkled. "What flowers?" He wasn't an actor and, honestly, he couldn't have made up that reaction.

"Are you horsing around with me?" Her frustration growing, she needed to be sure.

He raised his hands, palms up. "Honest. I don't have a clue what you're talking about. It wasn't me." Now he looked curious. "You got flowers and no one signed their name?"

She nodded, racking her brain to figure out who besides Joe would do such a thing.

Now he looked perturbed. "You must have an admirer."

"Oh, come on." Where did he get off, making such crazy statements?

"You don't think guys watch you?"

"I'm *pregnant*, Joe."

"You wear those baggy scrubs, and you're only just now starting to really show."

"You've got to be kidding. I don't encourage anyone. I mean I smile at people, I'm nice, but that's just being polite." If not Joe, then who? And, honestly, she was disappointed they hadn't been from him, and, she wanted to kick herself for even allowing the next thought.

Was that a look of jealousy on his face?

Joe hadn't felt this jealous in a long time. He'd skipped the jealous part with his wife, going directly to fury once he'd found out she'd gotten pregnant with Rico. But this was different. This feeling eating through his gut right now was good old-fashioned jealousy.

Who the hell had sent Carey flowers?

He looked suspiciously around the department. He'd introduced Frank to her at the party on the roof, but surely he could tell Carey and Joe were more than roommates. Plus they hadn't spoken two words to each other beyond, "Hi, how are you?"

It was time to get honest with himself. What could he expect? Carey was stunningly beautiful and he'd noticed admiring glances around the hospital whenever she passed by. At first it had given him great satisfaction to know she was living with him, and no one knew about it. It had been his big, fun secret. The gorgeous woman who'd come in as Jane Doe was his housemate. Now someone had the nerve to make a move on her. And it really ticked him off.

If—no, *when* he found out who it was he'd have an in-your-face moment and straighten out any misunderstanding. Carey was off-limits. Got that? Did he have

the right to do that? No. But he felt unreasonable whenever things involved her, and he was being honest with
himself. He. Was. Jealous.

"Um, I've got to get back to work. My shift's almost
over," she said.

"Sure. Okay. If I find out anything, I'll let you know."

"Thanks."

He watched her leave, her hair high in a ponytail that
swayed with each step. When he noticed one of the ER
docs also watching her, he wanted to cuff the back of
the guy's head. Carey was off limits. Was he being ter-
ritorial when he had no right to be? Yes. Hell, yes. He
folded his arms across his chest, the anger soon turning to self-doubt. How could he honestly expect loyalty from Carey when he wasn't even prepared to come
clean with her about the truth of his past?

In a frustrated fit he flung his pencil across the desk.
His EMT lifted a single brow at him.

Don't dare ask, if you value your job.

Back home that night, the more Carey thought about
it, the more upset she got about the flowers. She tried
to remember giving anyone the slightest misconcep-
tion that she was interested. Beyond Joe, that was. But
what bothered her more was that Joe seeming to run
hot and cold with her. She still didn't put it past him to
send those flowers and pretend he hadn't. Surely he'd
noticed how down she'd been lately, since they'd been
forced to change their relationship. But wait, they hardly
saw each other anymore. Maybe he hadn't noticed anything about her mood swings.

One thing she knew for a fact, she'd gone and ruined
everything by kissing him and coming on to him that
night. She was a runaway, pregnant with another man's

baby. Did she expect Joe to be a saint on top of everything wonderful about him and welcome her into his life
with open arms? She should have left well enough alone.

She took the bouquet home and put the vase on the
coffee table in the center of the living room. Might as
well enjoy them since someone had spent a lot of money
on them. She chewed a nail and stared at the flowers.
Had their one incredible night together been worth all
the confusion and heartache it had caused?

She thought for a couple of seconds and shivered
through and through with some incredible memories.
Hell, yeah!

Dejected, she went to the bathroom and washed her
face and was getting ready for bed when she heard Joe
let himself into the house.

There was no way Joe could avoid those flowers
when he came in. They may not have been from him,
but they sure would be a perfect catalyst to force them
to have a long-overdue conversation about a few things.

She needed answers to the question that wouldn't
stop circling through her mind, especially since seeing how jealous he'd been earlier: *Where do we stand?*

He'd said he didn't know who had given the flowers to her, and had seemed not to care. He'd even sug-
gested that she'd unknowingly flirted with someone
and might have encouraged the gift, which really an-
noyed her. Like it was her fault. And come on, she was
pregnant! Why the hell would she want to get involved
with a new guy now?

Precisely! That was what he'd hinted at the night he'd
leveled with her. They had no business getting involved.

But she couldn't get Joe's expression out of her mind
from when she'd confronted him at work and he'd sworn
he hadn't been the one to send the flowers. It had been

a look of pure jealousy, until he'd quickly covered it up. He still had feelings for her, as she did for him.

What a mess.

All revved up, she headed straight for the living room and the man who'd just come home. "You know what I don't get?"

"Well, hello to you, too." He looked more tired than he usually did, coming off his shift, like maybe he hadn't been sleeping well. Join the club! Or maybe work had been more stressful than usual.

"If you don't want anything to do with me anymore, why were you jealous?"

"Jealous? What are you talking about?" Now, on top of looking tired, he looked confused.

"I saw your eyes when I told you about those flowers." She didn't need to point them out. He'd obviously seen them the instant he'd walked in. His demeanor shifted, having more to do with her accusation than the flowers.

"I'll admit, it took me by surprise. And I still don't like the idea of some guy hitting on you in such an obvious way."

"But you have no right to." She folded her arms across her chest, having just then remembered she was in her pajamas. "You made it very clear we aren't allowed to have feelings for each other. It's for the best. Remember?"

He went solemn, watching her, and she made it clear she intended to have it out right then and there. Too bad if he was tired or jealous or whatever else. Now was the time. Finally. "If you don't care about me, why were you jealous?"

In an instant he'd covered the distance between them, and his hands were on her shoulders, pulling her toward him. Time seemed to stand still for a moment as they looked deep into each other's eyes and both seemed to know—without the benefit of a single word, just using that damn communication thing they had going on—that once again they were about to do something they'd regret. But it didn't stop Joe from planting a breathtaking kiss on Carey. And it didn't stop Carey from kissing him back like it might be the last kiss she'd ever get in her life. From Joe.

The kiss extended for several seconds, turning into a getting-to-know-you-all-over-again kind of thing. Her breasts tingled and tightened as she felt the tension from Joe's fingers digging into her shoulders while he continued to claim her lips. With them, a kiss was *always* more than just a kiss. She sighed over his mouth, searching with her tongue, soon finding his.

Joe's breathing proved he was as moved as she was, but then just when they were getting to the really good part he stopped. And stared into her eyes, a combination of desire and seething in his.

"Because I *am* jealous. Damn it." He'd finished with her, and now gently pushed her away.

She felt foolish standing there, her breasts peaked and pushing against the thin material of her pajama top, exposing exactly what he'd just done to her. "You can't do this to me, Joe. I don't understand why you act this way. It's not fair to keep me all mixed up like this."

He looked back at her, considering what she'd just said, and then, as if he'd made a huge decision, his expression changed to one of determination. "Then you'd better sit down, because if you want to know why I'm the way I am, it's a long story."

The comment sent a shiver through her. He finally intended to open up to her, and she was suddenly afraid of what she might find out. But she cared about Joe, and if it meant helping her understand him, she'd listen to anything he needed to share. No matter how bad it was or hard to hear.

She took a seat on the edge of the small couch. Joe chose to pace the room.

"How far back do you want me to go?"

"To the beginning, if that helps explain things."

He stopped pacing, stared at his feet for a second or two, as if calculating how far back he needed to go to get his story told once and forever. Then he started. "I met Angela, my ex-wife, when I took my paramedic training in an extension course at UCLA. We started a study group and things heated up pretty fast. Within the year, once we both got our certifications and got jobs, we got married." He glanced up at Carey, who hadn't stopped watching him for an instant. "You know how I love my family." She nodded. "Well, since I was married I wanted to start having kids right off. Like my parents did. I'd launched my business and things were going well, so I figured, let's go for it."

He started moving around the room again, turning his back on her. "After a year she still hadn't gotten pregnant, and we wondered if our stressful jobs might have something to do with it. So we took a two-week vacation to Cancun. Still nothing." He cleared his throat and glanced sheepishly back at Carey. She continued to train her gaze on him, so he turned around and faced her. "We decided to get fertility tests done. But I've got to tell you, things were really tense between us around that time, too." His hand quickly scraped along his jaw. "You know how you hear stories all the time about people who can't have kids, then they adopt a kid and the woman gets pregnant?"

Carey nodded, her heart racing as he came to what she suspected would be a key part of his story.

"Well, Angela got pregnant." He lifted his hands. "Great, huh?"

Somehow she knew it hadn't been great.

"I was thrilled, of course, and we went on our merry way, planning to be parents."

She read anything but happiness in his words, and especially with the tension of his brows and tightening in his jaw she understood he was in pain. Wait a second, she also knew Angela had left him for his best friend. He'd told her that much. But with his baby? Oh, my God, how horrible. And here she'd been dragging him to her parenting classes! If she'd only known.

Making him repeat the entire history for her benefit was cruel. "Joe, you don't have to—"

"Nope. I said I would, and I want you to hear the whole mess. Okay?" He looked pointedly at her, like it was her fault for making him begin and she needed to hear him out.

Carey tried to relax her shoulders but felt the tension fan across her chest instead. "Okay. Go on, then." She could barely breathe in anticipation.

"So we're all thrilled and planning for our baby and five months into the whole thing, out of the blue my fertility results show up in the mail. We'd completely forgotten about them because we were pregnant!" He made a mocking gesture of excitement, and it came off as really angry. "Where they'd been all that time, I didn't have a clue, but, bam, one day the results were there. Angela wasn't home when I opened them." He stopped, needing to swallow again. "And the thing is, it turned out..." He glanced up quickly, if possible look-

ing even more in pain, and then, dipping his head, his
eyes darted away. "I'm sterile."

How could that be? He was a healthy, magnificent
specimen of a man, but she knew to keep her thoughts
to herself.

"I did some research after I got that diagnosis because, honestly, I couldn't believe it. Evidently my
sperm ducts are defective from multiple injuries in high-
school baseball and from kick boxing. It's the only explanation the doctor could come up with when I finally
followed up. Who knew high-school sports could do a
guy in?"

Carey stared hard at Joe as she bit her lip, hoping her
eyes wouldn't well up. Angela had been pregnant and
living a lie under his roof. Of course, now she understood why her being pregnant seemed difficult for Joe.
Oh, God, what he'd been through. And she'd rubbed his
nose in that memory every single day she'd lived here.
She wanted to cross the room and hug him then apol-
ogize, but every unspoken message he sent said, *Stay
away. Leave me alone. Let me get this out once and for
all. You asked for it!* So she stayed right where she was,
aching for him and crying on the inside.

"My life stopped right then. All the happy future-
parents hoopla came crashing down. My wife was
pregnant—but not by me." His words were agitated and
the pacing started up again. Carey understood how hard
this must be for Joe, but he insisted he needed to tell
the entire story. So he paced on, and she waited, nearly
holding her breath. "I thought it had to be a mistake. I
called the fertility clinic, suggesting they'd mixed things
up. They'd obviously lost my results, since it had taken
so long to mail them. But, nope, I was one hundred per

cent sterile. Said so right there on that piece of paper."
He flashed her a sad, half-dead excuse for a smile.

"So I had to confront my wife." He'd lowered his
voice as if this part was solemn, or someone had died.
"Angela insisted it was a mistake, because I hadn't
told her I'd already called to make sure. I watched her
squirm and avoid looking at me. I never felt so sick in
my life." Joe gave a pained, ironic laugh. "Oh, she swore
the baby was ours, that it had to be. I listened to her
lie. Then she finally broke down and confessed that if
the baby wasn't ours it was Rico's." Joe's fist smashed
into the palm of his other hand. Carey started to understand the importance of his punching bag. Yet all she
wanted to do was rush to him, hold him and kiss him.
He'd been betrayed by the two most important people
in his life after his family.

"My best freaking friend." A hand shot to his forehead, fingers pinching his temples as if he'd suddenly
gotten a headache, reliving the story. He sucked in a
ragged breath. "Evidently, just before we'd gone to Cancun, when things had gotten really intense here, she'd
gone to him to cry on his shoulder, but a hell of a lot
more than that wound up happening. Turns out my *best*
friend had an unusual way of consoling *my* wife."

Anger and sarcasm mixed as his agitation grew. She
wanted to tell him to stop, not say anything else, but
kept silent, sensing his need to purge the full story at
long last.

"Angela swore she'd been too racked with guilt to
tell me, especially when she didn't know who the real
father was. Can you believe it? If she could have gotten away with it, she would have tried. And I got to
think I was the future father of a beautiful baby for five

months before we were forced to face the facts. What a fool I'd been."

Carey shook her head, feeling responsible for his pain right now. "You don't have to say anything else, Joe."

"But wait, it only gets better! Angela told Rico and he wanted her to get a paternity test! Yeah, he turned out to be a real prince. So there I was looking at this stranger who was supposed to be my wife, and she's telling me about this bastard who was *supposed* to be my best friend, and the only thing I could think of saying was, 'You can leave now. You're welcome to each other.' Yet part of me couldn't bear to kick out a pregnant woman, and I was about to take it back when she got up and called Rico." A look of incredulity covered his face. "Right in front of me she told him I knew everything, and she needed a place to stay."

Joe nailed Carey with his tortured expression. "They've been together ever since. Have a baby girl and seem to be doing fine. Or at least that's what I hear from other people I used to know."

Carey's hand flew to her chest. Joe had lost his wife, child and best friend in a single moment. And to make matters worse, he also knew he'd never be able to have a child of his own. What torture that must have been for a guy who'd wanted a big family. Yet when she glanced at him she saw a man suddenly at peace.

"As you can imagine, relationships have been off-limits for me for a while now. I mean, what's the point? I'm not into one-night stands, and I can't give a woman what she'd want most if we got serious—children of her own. Not unless I send her over to Rico."

"That's not funny, Joe." Carey had heard enough, and she'd realized why Joe was the distant man he was for so many reasons. Why he blew hot and cold. It went against his natural personality to be bitter, though, which had always confused her, but now she understood why. "I'm so sorry this happened to you. Now I see why you overreacted to me getting those flowers. I mean, it makes perfect sense…"

"Nothing *ever* makes perfect sense, Carey." He sounded desperate, tired and defeated. He went into the kitchen and filled a glass with tap water, then drank. She followed him there, wishing she could love away his sadness and anger, yet understanding why he deserved to feel that way. Why he needed to keep her at a distance.

"Then I show up on your doorstep pregnant and homeless, and you're too nice a guy to toss me out. I get it. The last thing I should have done was come on to you, but I believed and still believe that it's mutual attraction. There's something real between us, Joe. You couldn't have faked that night."

He swung around, some of the water slopping out of the glass. "It doesn't matter what happened that night. It can't ever happen again. There's no point. Besides, you're all set up now. You've got a job, an income, you're back on your feet—hell, someone even sent you flowers."

"Joe, that's uncalled for."

"Is it? Ever heard the phrase 'been there done that'? I can't do it again. Won't."

Pain clutched her chest when she realized what he intended to do. Every secret hope she'd held on to was about to get dashed by a guy who'd been beaten up by love and never wanted to open his heart or life to love again.

"Look, Carey, you're a strong woman who knows

what's best for you and the baby." Now he sounded like he was pleading for her to let him go. For her not to torment him by dangling love and sex in front of him by living under his roof. "You'll be an amazing mother. Truth is, you don't need me anymore. You're ready to move on."

"Please don't push us away..." her lip trembled as she spoke from being so racked with emotion "...because you're afraid you'll get pushed first. I'm not that girl. I'm not Angela."

"And I'm not the guy for you. Sorry."

He'd shut down completely, going against every single thing she knew in her soul about him. He wanted to be the scarred guy who could never feel again, but he lied. She'd seen and felt his love firsthand. He hated that his wife had once lied to him, but now he was lying to *her*. He wanted her to leave, and she couldn't argue with a man who'd just turned to stone in front of her eyes.

"Please listen, Joe."

Something snapped. Anguish mixed with fury flashed in his stare. "Don't you get it? Every time I look at you I'm reminded what I can never have for myself. I may be stuck in the Dark Ages, but I can't get past that."

She'd heard his deepest hurt. Joe had pretended, but he really hadn't survived his wife cheating on him with his best friend, on top of finding out he was sterile. That was a total life game changer; he was broken and she couldn't fix it. He'd just said her presence only made the pain worse.

He may as well have stabbed her, and the jolt of reality nearly sent her reeling backwards. Lashing out, he'd wanted to wound her, too, and he'd done a fine job. Her eyes burned and her hands shook.

She'd promised herself she'd never beg a man the

way her mother used to beg her father. And even though her world, the new and improved version of her world since she'd come to California and met Joe, had just been ripped from her, she wouldn't beg.

A sudden surge of anger and pride made her jaw clamp shut and her shoulders straighten. Joe was damaged and wasn't open to reason. There was just no point in trying to get through to him. "I'll be out by the end of the week."

She could scarcely believe her own words, but now that she'd said them she'd have to make sure she'd carry them out. No matter what.

CHAPTER NINE

NEXT WEEK AT WORK, Carey still reeled from her final confrontation with Joe. They'd been avoiding each other like a deadly disease ever since. What a mess. She'd promised to be gone by the end of the week, and had put the word out with the nurses on her floor for any leads on small apartments to rent.

She sat in a corner, scrolling through all of her assigned patients' labs for the day, insisting on giving them her full attention. Afterwards, she'd do her morning patient assessments then pass their meds. Sometimes putting her life on hold for her day job was a relief.

"Carey?" Dr. Di Williams stood behind her.

"Yes? Anything you need, Dr. Williams?"

The middle-aged doctor offered a kind smile. "I hear there's something *you* need."

Carey quirked her brow. "Sorry?"

"An apartment?"

"Oh. Yes, well, something will pan out, I'm sure." She prayed it would because it was Wednesday and she'd promised Joe she'd be out by the weekend at the latest.

"I've got an in-law suite at my house. No one ever

uses it. It's got a private entrance and even a small kitchen. It's yours if you'd like it."

A few people were beginning to realize she was pregnant. Unfortunately, Stephanie had seen her go to the Parentcraft class, so probably the whole clinic knew by now. Obviously, Dr. Williams knew from when Carey had been her patient. "That's very kind of you, but—"

"It's a nice place. My partner and I have a house right here in the Hollywood Hills. Lisa made sure the place was comfortable and inviting, but her parents won't come to visit, and I've given up on mine coming around for years now. So what I'm saying is you're welcome to live there. I know you've had a rough time and I'd like to help you out."

Touched to her core, Carey jumped up and hugged Dr. Williams, who looked both surprised and uncomfortable. "You're a godsend. Thank you."

It was the first time Carey had ever seen the doctor grin. "We thought about adopting once, but our jobs are so demanding we decided it wouldn't be fair to the baby. Plus we're both, well, you know, getting older." She gave a self-deprecating smile. "So we'll enjoy meeting your bambino when the time comes."

She patted Carey's stomach, and Carey fully realized the reality that, yes, her baby would be born, and that after tomorrow, when she'd had another sonogram, maybe she'd even know the sex. Which made ner think how Joe had always called her baby little Spencer. It hit her then. She *really* needed a place to live. She was ready to "nest," as she'd learned the word in her parenting class. She wanted this, and the good doctor had just solved her problem.

"But I have to insist on paying rent."

Dr. Williams tossed her a gaze that perfectly expressed her thoughts—*Please, I'm a rich doctor and do we really have to negotiate money when we're having such a good moment?* "Whatever you want to pay is fine. Money isn't an issue for us. In case you didn't know, Lisa's a doctor, too."

"I'll be in great company." Carey beamed while she talked, never having felt more grateful in her life. Well, after her unending indebtedness to Joe, of course. She gave an amount she felt she could afford, nothing close to what the place would be worth, she was pretty much sure of that. But she was being honest, though, not wanting to insult the doctor by going too low, since she'd have to live on a tight budget. Especially as she'd have to return the rental car soon and would need to find a used car for transportation. *One step at a time, Carey.* Thank goodness she'd banked some unused vacation time at her hospital back in Chicago and they'd sent the final check to Joe's address last week.

"That works for me," Di said. "I'll bring the key tomorrow and you can start moving in right away."

The doctor turned to walk away, but Carey grabbed her hand and shook it, well, over-shook it, because she wanted to make her point. "You and Lisa are lifesavers. Thank you, thank you, thank you."

"Like I said, it'll be fun." Before right this moment fun would never have been a word she would have associated with Dr. Di Williams. Who knew?

Along with the warmth Carey felt for the incredible kindness of others, especially from Joe, and now from a woman Carey hardly knew, she felt new hope for her and her baby. She just might be able to pull this off, start a new life in California and move on from her past once and for all. One sad and nagging point kept her from full elation.

Joe.

She loved the guy. And she'd never get to tell him. But she'd learned her lesson in life well. Just because you wanted something, it didn't mean you'd get it. It would be too much to ask of him to love her and to accept her child, too. Not after everything he'd been through. She understood that now.

She sighed, a bittersweet thought about leaving Joe's sweet little house for her new and as yet unseen place nearly making her cry. She'd gotten so used to living with him she hated thinking about not seeing him every day. Was this really happening? Maybe she was still in a coma and this was one big Alice-in-Wonderland-style dream. The thought amused her briefly.

But she had labs to look at, and one of her assigned patients had just put on their call light.

Thank heavens for the distraction of her day job.

In order to avoid Carey and every disturbing thought she dredged up in him, Joe worked several extra shifts during the last week she lived with him. On Friday he'd even stayed on for an extra night shift so he wouldn't chance seeing her move out. The thought of watching her go would only widen the gaping wound inside him.

He'd finally opened up and told her everything, and she'd seen how messed up he truly was. Even then he'd felt her need to comfort him, but he'd held her off, pushed her away, then, once she'd seen there was just no point, that he'd never let her in, she'd agreed to move out. Whatever they'd once shared had breathed its last breath, and all the CPR in the world couldn't revive it.

It had been a crazy evening on the job with nonstop calls, and truthfully, Joe was grateful for the constant distraction.

James had thought of everything when he'd set up the hospital for his private and exclusive clientele. One perk was an emergency box in every home that went directly to The Hills emergency department instead of the more general Los Angeles system.

At two a.m. another call came through, this one from an affluent area, the Los Feliz Hills, east of The Hollywood Hills Clinic. A woman reported her husband in sudden pain that was shooting down his left arm. The emergency operator sent the message to Joe and he grabbed his team and hit the road within two minutes, siren switched on.

The five-mile distance would take fifteen minutes, thanks to the winding roads in both of the hilly communities. While they drove, the emergency operator stayed on the line and gave instructions to the wife of the patient, in case she needed to begin CPR.

Once in front of the ornate house Joe's team grabbed their emergency kits and EMT Benny rolled in the stretcher. A young housekeeper waited at the front door to the huge several-storied home and directed them up an open stairwell to the master bedroom. Joe couldn't help but notice the largest chandelier he thought he'd ever seen in a home. He quickly recalled the Hills ER operator having mentioned that the patient was the head of one of the movie studios in town.

Joe found the white-haired patient on the floor, unconscious, his wife kneeling over him in near panic.

"He just passed out," she said, fear painting a frightened mask on her face.

"Does he have a history of coronary artery disease?"

She nodded.

Joe rushed to the patient's side, finding him unresponsive. He checked his airway and found him to be breathing, then he checked his carotid artery for a pulse.

"Let's get him on the stretcher," Joe directed his team, taking out the portable four-lead ECG machine and hooking up the patient for an initial reading as they applied oxygen and rolled him onto the adjustable stretcher. Then, in an effort to save more precious time, he started the IV as they transported the man down that huge stairwell. Once that IV was in place, he checked the initial four-lead heart strip, which showed possible ST elevation. Once Benny and his partner got the patient in the back of the emergency van, Joe jumped in, immediately switching the man to the twelve-lead EKG for a more thorough reading. Applying the leads, Joe was grateful the old guy wore loose-fitting pajamas, making his job a little easier.

Time was of the essence with MIs and seconds after securing the stretcher in the safety lock in the back of the van Benny and the other EMT shot to the front, turned on the emergency lights but not the siren, as a courtesy not to add stress to the heart patient, and sped down the winding hills.

Now with proof the man was in the midst of a STEMI, thanks to the twelve-lead EKG but still maintaining a decent enough blood pressure—he was even coming around a little bit, giving occasional moans— Joe added a nitroglycerin IV piggyback, gave him morphine through the IV line and aspirin under his tongue. He might not be able to stop the ST elevation myocardial infarction, but he hoped to at least help decrease the patient's pain. All this was done while the ambulance tossed and rolled around the hills, heading for Los Feliz Boulevard and onward toward Hollywood and the clinic.

Without the benefit of lab reports, he couldn't treat the patient more aggressively. And since the definitive treatment for an MI was catheterization, Joe's one job was to keep the guy alive.

The man looked ashen and his breathing had become more difficult. Joe repositioned his head for better airway and increased the oxygen one liter. oxygen sats stank. Then he checked his blood pressure, which was even lower than previously, but assumed it could be due to the nitro and morphine.

The heart monitor started alarming. Damn it, the guy was crashing. At times like these Joe felt frustrated with his role as a gap-filler until the patient got to the ER and could be hit with all the fancy lifesaving drugs. If only the ambulance could get there faster.

When the monitor went to flatline, Joe immediately started CPR, and continued to do so for the last five minutes of the ride to the clinic and the ambulance entrance where the medical big guns waited.

Unfortunately for the patient, medically the future didn't look too bright. In an oddball nonmedical way, Joe could relate.

Joe parked the car in his garage, closed the door, and headed into his house from the backyard entrance on Saturday morning. He hated how the house had felt since Carey had moved out yesterday. Had it only been yesterday? It seemed more like a month or a year even since he'd last seen her. Before, there had been this incredible life force radiating from her room. Today all he felt when he walked near it was his energy getting zapped by pain and regret. Well, he planned to save himself the angst and head right to his room to sleep.

After the stress of that morning, with the Hollywood

movie tycoon who'd wound up dying despite all emergency measures, he felt dejected and needed to sleep. It seemed typical of issues of the heart, and maybe even a metaphor for his own life lately, especially where his relationship with Carey was concerned, and with all the practical training in the world he still couldn't fix his own messed-up heart. Come to think of it, he might tear a page from Carey's story—a short-term coma would be a good thing right about now.

As usual, with any downtime, Carey was foremost on his mind. The word "coma" brought unwanted thoughts about a lady he'd once sat vigil for at her bedside. What had he done? He'd lost her. Sent her away. He unloaded the contents of his cargo pockets onto his dresser top then dug out his cell phone.

Wait a second. He'd worked all night and hadn't turned on his personal phone so he'd missed a text from Carey. He was so tired he squinted to read it.

It's a girl. Latest sonogram. Yes!

The words nearly brought him to his knees. Little Spencer was a girl. Carey didn't have anyone in her life to share the news with but him. A sudden feeling of sadness punched his gut. He'd been so selfishly focused he hadn't considered what moving out had meant for her. She'd volunteered to go and, like a wuss, he'd let her.

She deserved so, so much more. Yet, with all the bad things life had dealt her, she insisted on being upbeat. Yes! she'd written. The text was short but so touching, and all he wanted to do was find her and hold her and tell her how he really felt.

It wasn't going to happen. It wasn't possible.

He should leave well enough alone.

His house had never felt so big or empty since she'd moved out. Only yesterday! Damn, it already felt like a year. How would he go on without her?

"You did the right thing," he said aloud, glancing into the mirror above his dresser. He had to believe it because otherwise he'd go crazy. He was so messed up. Carey and the baby only would have left at some point anyway, so it was better it had happened sooner rather than later, and as *his* idea, not hers. In a childish way he admitted it felt better to have forced the change because he couldn't have survived Carey leaving him. By his spin, sending her away had been the most unselfish thing he'd done in his life.

Besides, she deserved a man with more to offer, someone without baggage like his. Anger, mistrust, suspicion, yeah, he was good at those sorry emotions. She'd had all of that tossed in her face long before she'd met him, beginning with her father and ending with that scumbag Ross. It was Carey's time to catch a break. He'd given it to her by pushing her out the door. Because he knew she was the special kind of woman who would have stuck around, put up with his sorry attitude, and tried to make the best of things if he hadn't made her leave. Beyond a laundry list of the ways she'd be better off without him, the main reason still stood out. He'd come around enough to know that Carey was nothing like Angela. He could trust what she said and did. She was as stable as they came, despite her tough life before coming to L.A. The issue was still with him.

He thought about her ultrasound and the fact her baby was a girl. The crux of the matter was that he would never know what it was like to have a woman he loved carry his baby. A kid who might look like him. And he was too damn messed up to get over it.

Better to set her free now before it got even more difficult because, honestly, he hadn't been prepared for the level of pain her leaving had unleashed. Sometimes he could barely breathe.

He thought about what he'd said to her the other night and cringed. He'd been harsh, insisting he couldn't get past his wife cheating on him, and he'd held it against a completely innocent person. What sense did that make?

He flopped, back first, onto his mattress, hands behind his head, praying sleep would find him and put him out of this torture, if only for a few hours. He'd tried to make peace with his decision about letting Carey go, but deep down something still didn't feel right.

Why, even now—when she'd found a great place to live, from what he'd heard floating around at work, and when she had nothing but good things to look forward to, a solid job, the upcoming arrival of her little baby girl, a bright future—things didn't feel right to him.

Why did he still have the foreboding sense she needed his protection?

He squeezed his eyes tight. *Go to sleep. Just go to sleep. You're getting delusional from lack of rest.*

He was bound to settle down soon because his body was completely drained and his mind so weary he could barely put two coherent thoughts together. Yeah, he'd get some sleep today, he promised himself. But first he needed a glass of water. So he hopped off the bed and headed to the kitchen for a drink.

Carey wanted to scold herself for accidentally taking Lori's clothes along with her when she'd packed the few meager possessions she owned and had moved out. Joe's sister had been nice enough to loan her some jeans and tops when she'd first moved in with zero belongings left to her name. Now she'd have to face him again, as painful as that would be, to return them. Truth was it had hurt to the core when he hadn't even bothered to reply to her text about her baby being a girl. She guessed he'd already moved on. Didn't care. Hadn't he said all she did was remind him of what he'd never have?

An ache burrowed deeply into her chest, not only for herself but for him, too. She still loved the guy. Had she imagined every good thing about Joe, or was this just how it felt to lose him? She was positive she'd never get over him, and had missed him every second since she'd moved out.

Mid-morning, she parked the rental car across the street from his house on the small cul-de-sac, thinking the car was another topic she had to bring up with Joe. As soon as she found a used car she could afford, she'd make sure this one got returned to Mr. Matthews. She wanted to make sure Joe knew she didn't expect to keep this car forever. Just for a little longer. She promised.

She reached around to the backseat and grabbed the tote bag with Lori's clothes inside. Carey had gotten the bag from the clinic the day she'd been discharged and Joe had taken her in. She'd almost slipped up and thought "home" the day when Joe had taken her home. Because that was how it'd felt when she'd walked through that door with him. She glanced at the small sage-green house across the street. Yes, he'd been a stranger then, but he'd saved her life and then kept vigil beside her hospital bed, and she'd never felt more protected or safe in her life than when she'd lived with him.

With the bag in her hand, she got out of the car and battled a feeling of half hope and half fear that Joe would be home. She'd left her house key the night she'd moved out. If he wasn't home now, she'd leave the items on the porch and make a quick getaway. On second thoughts, he'd been working so much it was possible he was sleeping and the last thing she wanted to do was wake him up. Maybe she'd just leave the bag on the lounger on his deck and not even attempt to face him right now. If she snuck off without seeing him, she'd save her lovelorn heart a whole lot of grief.

She started down the driveway, getting halfway to the kitchen-window area when she caught herself. This was cowardly. She was a big girl now. She needed to face him if he was home, though there was no sign of his car so she made a one-eighty-degree turn and headed back toward the front of the house, stunned to find a man she'd never expected to see again only a few feet away.

Ross.

How had he found her? How had he known where she'd been living? A chill zipped down her spine and her stomach felt queasy.

Then it hit her. He was the one who'd sent the flow-ers. How had he…? Oh, wait, he knew how to manipu-late people, especially women, and had probably gotten the work address out of Polly in the employee relations department back in Chicago. Carey had been in touch with her regularly since she'd arrived in Hollywood— first to let the hospital know about her situation and to take a leave of absence, then to set up receiving her backdated pay checks, and eventually to give notice on the job and to collect her unused vacation pay. What a fool she'd been to think he wouldn't find her.

She'd thought she'd been so careful, but nothing seemed to be beyond Ross's reach. The bastard. After the quick flash of fear at seeing him she went directly into anger. The creep had another thought coming if he planned to mess up her life again. She was in control now, in no small part thanks to Joe, and Ross was powerless.

He kept his distance. Even held his hands up, all the while watching her, like a prowling animal waiting to pounce. "I know what you're probably thinking," he said, trying to sound appeasing. "What am I doing here?" He gave a poor excuse for a smile that looked more like an insincere politician's than a former lover's.

"I don't want to see you. Leave. Now."

Quickly his expression changed to that of a mistreated puppy. "I'm sorry. I've come to tell you I'm sorry. I love you. We can still be happy together. Make a life together."

"Ha! That's rich. You wanted me to get rid of my baby. That's not going to happen. There's nothing further to talk about."

She looked at Ross, tall, dark, and had she really used to think he was handsome? All he looked like now was a creep she needed to get rid of. Fast. He'd abused her, both mentally and physically. Had wanted her to have an abortion, had shoved money into her hand to do it, too.

She thought about Ross's polar opposite, Joe, and all he'd tried to do for her. How hard it must have been for him to show up at the prenatal appointments, to be the first one she shared the first sonogram with, when never being able to become a father had still been eating away at him. The moment he'd slid into that chair beside her in the parenting class had nearly made her heart burst with gratitude. He'd acted the part of being a father, even when he'd believed he would lose her and the baby, as if his past was bound to repeat itself. Yet he'd shown up and stuck with it, for her, and had never let on about the pain he must have suffered because of it. Oh, God, he was her true hero—a man to be worshipped, adored and loved. With all of her heart. And she did. She loved him.

Facing Ross, right now, she knew without a doubt what her true feelings were for Joe. Yet Joe had convinced her to walk out on him. And she'd gone because he'd looked so tortured by her being there.

She stood before Ross, a shadow of a man standing by the driveway hedge, feeling completely alone. All she wanted to do was go inside Joe's house where she'd always felt safe, and close and lock the door. Forever. On Ross.

She kept her distance, not trusting him for one second, but Ross took a single step forward.

She'd never let herself be a victim again and he'd have to hear her out. "You need to know I've finally experienced a good relationship. I know for a fact there are good, loving and caring men in the world who put their partners first. I never learned that from you, but now I have faith in the world again. In myself." She touched her heart. "You wanted to control me and tear me down to keep me under your thumb. I may have let you before but I never will again." To show how serious she was, and to prove she wasn't afraid of him anymore, she took a step forward but still kept safely out of his reach, then stared him down. "You need to leave L.A. I'll never go back to you. Never."

Ross's expectant-puppy expression soon turned to one of defeat. Did he think he could just show up and everything would be fine again? Was he that out of touch with reality? Or had it proved once and for all how he truly had zero respect for her.

Something she'd said must have gotten through to him because he actually turned to leave. Carey took a breath for the first time in several seconds. But just as quickly he turned back, lunging toward her with the look of pure rage in his demon eyes.

His first mistake had been showing up uninvited in California. His second mistake was to grab her wrist and clamp down hard enough to cut off her blood supply, then raise his other hand ready to slap her.

Instead of pulling away, fighting mad, Carey growled and steamrolled into him. Catching him off guard, her knee connected full force with his groin, the V of her free hand ramming with all her might smack into his larynx. Everything Joe had taught her about self-defense came rushing back with a vengeance.

Ross doubled over in pain, unable to gasp or shout. And, of course, he'd let go of her wrist. Shocked she'd actually pulled it off, Carey stood there dazed for one second, her body covered in goose bumps, staring at him while he writhed in pain on the driveway.

Well, plan A had worked like a charm. What was she supposed to do next?

Run! Run for the car and get the hell out of there. She turned to make her getaway, but slammed into a brick wall of a man.

CHAPTER TEN

JOE CAME FLYING out of the kitchen door the instant he'd seen the man lunge for Carey. He'd watched the whole encounter between the guy who must be Ross and Carey, the woman he loved and his new superhero, from the window above the kitchen sink.

He'd known Carey needed to face down her demon once and for all, and he'd been ready to pounce if she'd needed him. So, as hard as it had been, he'd stayed on the ready just around the corner and waited. She'd stood up to the man, not wavering for a second. When twisted reasoning hadn't panned out, the guy had lunged at her. Joe had rushed through the back door and flown outside, but she'd beaten him to the punch. Like a pro, she'd taken down her attacker. It had impressed the hell out of Joe, too. Great going.

Pride for Carey mixed with pure fear that she could have been hurt by the bastard from her past made him take her in his arms and hold tight. She didn't fight it either, just leaned into him.

"You okay?"

She nodded, then pulled back to look into his eyes. "Did you see that? I decked him! Thanks to you."

He laughed, all the while watching Ross, who slowly began to get onto his hands and knees.

"Do as Carey says, just stand up and leave. Don't ever come back," he said, with Carey safely tucked under one arm, ready, if necessary to take the matter into his own hands if the guy made so much as a hint of a move in the wrong direction.

Now Ross stood, anger still plainly carved in his face.

"The police will be here shortly," Joe said. "I called when I first saw you. She's also got a restraining order out on you in case you ever get any ideas about coming around again. Consider it your 'go-straight-to-jail' card and this is your final warning."

Ross took one look at Joe, saw the don't-even-think-about-messing-with-me stare and took off, running to the street and back toward Santa Monica Boulevard.

With arms still wrapped around each other, they watched him disappear round the corner.

"I don't have a restraining order out on him," Carey said.

"He doesn't know that."

"And the police, are they coming?"

"Again, he doesn't need to know I was just about to call when I saw you kick his ass, so I hung up to help you." Joe flashed Carey a proud grin. "You were the bomb, babe."

She laughed. "You taught me everything I know."

He pulled her near and hugged her tight. God, he'd missed her. To think he'd almost let her get away sent shivers through his chest. "You're all right? Let me see your wrist, it looked like he had a firm grip." He checked out the area around her thin wrist, which was reddened and showing signs of early bruising. Like a dope, he kissed it because it was the only thing he could think to do, and he wanted more than anything for Carey to understand how precious she was to him. "You need to know something. I said things the other night that were horrible and not true. The only person you remind me of is you, and I never want to lose you. Or your daughter."

She disengaged her wrist from his hands so she could stroke his cheek. Looking into his eyes with her soft green stare, she smiled. He got the distinct message she had a few things to clear up with him, too.

"I never want to lose you either. Standing up to Ross just now made me realize he was the one who should feel ashamed, not me. That dark past I dragged out here needs to stay in Chicago with that loser. It shouldn't have any influence over me or my future. I've started over again. That ugly shadow is gone for good."

He believed her, too. She stood before him a woman of conviction, nothing like the frightened victim he'd first met two months ago.

She went up on her toes and delivered a light kiss. He matched it with a kiss of his own, and damn if it didn't feel like a little piece of heaven had just tiptoed back into his life.

"I meant what I said to him, too," she said, her arms lightly resting around his neck. "You've given me faith again in love. You helped me learn that it's not weak to open myself up to someone and to love again. Even if you didn't want me to." Her eyes dipped down for a second then swept back up. "I couldn't stop myself from loving you. I do, Joe, I love you."

Now he felt like the coward, well, until five minutes ago anyway, when he'd watched Carey confront her biggest fear and kick its ass, and Joe finally knew without a doubt that he loved her, too. No matter how hard he'd tried, he hadn't been able to stop himself from falling in love with her. He'd pulled out every old and sorry reason to keep from loving her, but she was meant to be loved, and he was the guy to do it. And for someone whose thoughts sounded suspiciously like a caveman's—*Me Joe. You Carey. We love.*—he had yet to voice the most important words he'd ever say. He just stood there, staring into her eyes, stroking her hair, loving her in silence.

"It's especially nice when you love someone." She cleared her throat to draw his attention away from her eyes and back to noticing all of her. "If that someone loves you back."

Hint, hint! There was that tiny mischievous smile she'd occasionally given when making an obvious point, and he'd missed it so much.

The ball was clearly in his court, and it was time for him to say what he felt and mean what he said. Without a doubt he loved Carey. So, still being in caveman mode, he bent down, swept her up into his arms and carried her up the steps to his front door.

Once inside he planted another kiss on her, and got the kind of reception he'd hoped for. But he knew he couldn't get away with a mere display of affection. If ever a person deserved, or a time called for, words, it was now. So he gently released her legs to the ground, snuck in one last quickie kiss, and stepped back.

"Please forgive me for pushing you away. I was hurt. And afraid. Still am. And if you don't think that's a huge thing for me to admit, you don't know me like you think you do."

"I totally understand how huge that is." She groped around his shoulders and chest. "Just like the rest of you."

He went along with her making light of things, because the topic was difficult and heavy and loaded with old habits that needed to be set free. They'd both been through so much lately, but he had one more thing to say and he needed to say it now. He cupped her face between his hands.

"I'll understand if you can't see a future with me, because I'm sterile and I can't make babies with you."

"Stop right there," she said. "You really don't get it, do you? Did you not hear me say I love you? You may not be the biological father of the little lady here, but you've acted nothing short of a true, loving, and beyond decent father. Actions really do speak louder than, well, other actions in this case, I guess." She screwed up her face in a perfectly adorable way, having briefly confused herself. Right now there wasn't a single thing she could do wrong. "I know, terrible analogy."

He laughed lightly, while understanding exactly what she'd meant, because that was part of what was so right about them, they always *got* what each other meant, spoken or not.

"But it's all the family we need," she added, and he loved her even more for her generous thought. But the truth was a small family could never be his style, that's why he'd decided to never be in the position to have a family at all. Until Carey had shown up and changed everything.

"You don't want her—what are we going to name her?—to have sisters and brothers? How about Peaches?"

"Name my daughter after a piece of fruit?" she playfully protested.

"Our daughter, you just said it, so that gives me equal naming privileges. Besides, I thought Peaches might be significant since I'm planning to make the famous Matthews ice cream just for you after dinner tonight."

"You're making me peach ice cream?"

"How else can I make sure you'll never leave me again?"

"Ah, your father's secret ingredient."

"Yes. That. Plus the fact you have no idea what a hellhole it's been here since you left, and I'll never let you go again."

"And…?" she encouraged him.

"Because I love you and can't imagine my life without you." He kissed her again, because there was no way he could say what he just had without needing to touch her, with the best expression of love he knew. Physical touch.

"Neither can I," she said. "And if we want to give, well, I'll agree to give her the nickname of Peaches, but honestly we'll have to come up with something better than that for real. Anyway, if we want to give her siblings in the future, first one step at a time and all, right? Let's see how this little one turns out. But, honestly, in this day and age, if we want more children, we can find a million ways to do it. Right?"

"Right, as usual. Sorry I've been so dense about that topic for so long. I've been too busy wallowing in my pain."

"And *that* should never come into play with us again. Okay?"

"You got it. Because I intend to spend the rest of my life showing both of you how much I love you."

She sighed her joy and nuzzled into his neck, which felt fantastic. "That works out perfectly because I intend to spend the rest of the afternoon showing you exactly how much I love you."

For a guy who'd been up all night and who earlier could hardly keep his eyes open, Joe suddenly felt full of life, love, and, right this instant, intense desire. He pressed his nose into her hair and inhaled the smell of fresh coconut shampoo, thinking how he could contentedly spend the rest of his life simply doing this. He smiled widely, knowing she had a far better idea. "I like your plan."

She gave him a long and leisurely kiss in case there was any mistaking what her intentions were. He loved how well they communicated.

"For the record," she whispered into the shell of his ear, "you had me at homemade peach ice cream."

* * * * *

Look out for the next two great stories in
THE HOLLYWOOD HILLS CLINIC

TAMING HOLLYWOOD'S ULTIMATE PLAYBOY
by Amalie Berlin

and WINNING BACK HIS DOCTOR BRIDE
by Tina Beckett

Available July 2016

And if you missed where it all started, check out

SEDUCED BY THE HEART SURGEON
by Carol Marinelli

FALLING FOR THE SINGLE DAD
by Emily Forbes

TEMPTED BY HOLLYWOOD'S TOP DOC
by Louisa George

PERFECT RIVALS...
by Amy Ruttan

THE PRINCE AND THE MIDWIFE
by Robin Gianna

HIS PREGNANT SLEEPING BEAUTY
by Lynne Marshall

All available now!

MILLS & BOON®
Hardback – June 2016

ROMANCE

Bought for the Greek's Revenge	Lynne Graham
An Heir to Make a Marriage	Abby Green
The Greek's Nine-Month Redemption	Maisey Yates
Expecting a Royal Scandal	Caitlin Crews
Return of the Untamed Billionaire	Carol Marinelli
Signed Over to Santino	Maya Blake
Wedded, Bedded, Betrayed	Michelle Smart
The Surprise Conti Child	Tara Pammi
The Greek's Nine-Month Surprise	Jennifer Faye
A Baby to Save Their Marriage	Scarlet Wilson
Stranded with Her Rescuer	Nikki Logan
Expecting the Fellani Heir	Lucy Gordon
The Prince and the Midwife	Robin Gianna
His Pregnant Sleeping Beauty	Lynne Marshall
One Night, Twin Consequences	Annie O'Neil
Twin Surprise for the Single Doc	Susanne Hampton
The Doctor's Forbidden Fling	Karin Baine
The Army Doc's Secret Wife	Charlotte Hawkes
A Pregnancy Scandal	Kat Cantrell
A Bride for the Boss	Maureen Child

MILLS & BOON®
Large Print – June 2016

ROMANCE

Leonetti's Housekeeper Bride	Lynne Graham
The Surprise De Angelis Baby	Cathy Williams
Castelli's Virgin Widow	Caitlin Crews
The Consequence He Must Claim	Dani Collins
Helios Crowns His Mistress	Michelle Smart
Illicit Night with the Greek	Susanna Carr
The Sheikh's Pregnant Prisoner	Tara Pammi
Saved by the CEO	Barbara Wallace
Pregnant with a Royal Baby!	Susan Meier
A Deal to Mend Their Marriage	Michelle Douglas
Swept into the Rich Man's World	Katrina Cudmore

HISTORICAL

Marriage Made in Rebellion	Sophia James
A Too Convenient Marriage	Georgie Lee
Redemption of the Rake	Elizabeth Beacon
Saving Marina	Lauri Robinson
The Notorious Countess	Liz Tyner

MEDICAL

Playboy Doc's Mistletoe Kiss	Tina Beckett
Her Doctor's Christmas Proposal	Louisa George
From Christmas to Forever?	Marion Lennox
A Mummy to Make Christmas	Susanne Hampton
Miracle Under the Mistletoe	Jennifer Taylor
His Christmas Bride-to-Be	Abigail Gordon

MILLS & BOON®
Hardback – July 2016

ROMANCE

Di Sione's Innocent Conquest	Carol Marinelli
Capturing the Single Dad's Heart	Kate Hardy
The Billionaire's Ruthless Affair	Miranda Lee
A Virgin for Vasquez	Cathy Williams
Master of Her Innocence	Chantelle Shaw
Moretti's Marriage Command	Kate Hewitt
The Flaw in Raffaele's Revenge	Annie West
The Unwanted Conti Bride	Tara Pammi
Bought by Her Italian Boss	Dani Collins
Wedded for His Royal Duty	Susan Meier
His Cinderella Heiress	Marion Lennox
The Bridesmaid's Baby Bump	Kandy Shepherd
Bound by the Unborn Baby	Bella Bucannon
Taming Hollywood's Ultimate Playboy	Amalie Berlin
Winning Back His Doctor Bride	Tina Beckett
White Wedding for a Southern Belle	Susan Carlisle
Wedding Date with the Army Doc	Lynne Marshall
The Baby Inheritance	Maureen Child
Expecting the Rancher's Child	Sara Orwig
Doctor, Mummy...Wife?	Dianne Drake

MILLS & BOON®
Large Print – July 2016

ROMANCE

The Italian's Ruthless Seduction	Miranda Lee
Awakened by Her Desert Captor	Abby Green
A Forbidden Temptation	Anne Mather
A Vow to Secure His Legacy	Annie West
Carrying the King's Pride	Jennifer Hayward
Bound to the Tuscan Billionaire	Susan Stephens
Required to Wear the Tycoon's Ring	Maggie Cox
The Greek's Ready-Made Wife	Jennifer Faye
Crown Prince's Chosen Bride	Kandy Shepherd
Billionaire, Boss...Bridegroom?	Kate Hardy
Married for Their Miracle Baby	Soraya Lane

HISTORICAL

The Secrets of Wiscombe Chase	Christine Merrill
Rake Most Likely to Sin	Bronwyn Scott
An Earl in Want of a Wife	Laura Martin
The Highlander's Runaway Bride	Terri Brisbin
Lord Crayle's Secret World	Lara Temple

MEDICAL

A Daddy for Baby Zoe?	Fiona Lowe
A Love Against All Odds	Emily Forbes
Her Playboy's Proposal	Kate Hardy
One Night...with Her Boss	Annie O'Neil
A Mother for His Adopted Son	Lynne Marshall
A Kiss to Change Her Life	Karin Baine

MILLS & BOON®

Why shop at millsandboon.co.uk?

Each year, thousands of romance readers find their perfect read at millsandboon.co.uk. That's because we're passionate about bringing you the very best romantic fiction. Here are some of the advantages of shopping at www.millsandboon.co.uk:

* **Get new books first**—you'll be able to buy your favourite books one month before they hit the shops

* **Get exclusive discounts**—you'll also be able to buy our specially created monthly collections, with up to 50% off the RRP

* **Find your favourite authors**—latest news, interviews and new releases for all your favourite authors and series on our website, plus ideas for what to try next

* **Join in**—once you've bought your favourite books, don't forget to register with us to rate, review and join in the discussions

Visit **www.millsandboon.co.uk**
for all this and more today!